Chameleon's Death Dance

By BR Kingsolver

Cover art by Heather Hamilton-Senter

http://www.bookcoverartistry.com/

Copyright 2017 BR Kingsolver

⊕⊕⊕

License Notes

⊕⊕⊕

Other books by BR Kingsolver

The Chameleon Assassin Series
Chameleon Assassin
Chameleon Uncovered
Chameleon's Challenge
Chameleon's Death Dance

The Telepathic Clans Saga
The Succubus Gift
Succubus Unleashed
Broken Dolls
Succubus Rising
Succubus Ascendant

Other books
I'll Sing for my Dinner
Trust

Short Stories in Anthologies
Here, Kitty Kitty
Bellator

BRKingsolver.com
Facebook
Twitter

Table of Contents

Even a chameleon can be a target.

Libby makes her money as a thief and assassin, but a girl has to have a cover. To her surprise, her business installing security systems in 23rd century Toronto is taking off, as is her romance with Wil— North America's top cop.

Then an insurance company hires her to recover a fortune in stolen art and jewelry. Bring them the stolen goods and they'll pay an outrageous fee, no questions asked.

The Vancouver art scene is hot, in more ways than one. Billionaires compete for bragging rights, and they aren't picky who they deal with.

With big money and reputations on the line, Libby is on a collision course with the super-rich. When too many questions make the art thieves uncomfortable, one of the world's top assassins is hired to eliminate those who know too much— including Libby.

CHAPTER 1

Danielle Kincaid hit the Vancouver social scene with a splash. Variously called 'a breath of fresh air,' 'an arrogant bitch,' 'refreshingly open and intelligent,' 'a promiscuous slut,' 'a spoiled rich girl,' and probably a few dozen other labels—depending on the particular commenter's point of view—she was certainly prominent. In a city with entrenched, and some might say fossilized, upper-crust families dating back before The Fall, the Kincaid name gave her instant access to high society that no one could deny.

Scion of the industrial dynasty founded by Daniel Kincaid two hundred years before, Danielle was a tall, dark blonde girl in her mid-twenties, beautiful, educated, and uninhibited. That she was wildly wealthy went without saying. She was a Kincaid.

Daniel Kincaid had been a visionary. Founder of a computer software company in Scotland at the end of the twentieth century, he paid close attention to the scientists who foretold an environmental catastrophe as humanity polluted the planet and changed the climate. He expanded his business empire to Northern Ireland, and then to Canada.

His three sons and one daughter inherited their father's smarts and ambition, further expanding the business that became a dominant player in computer controls for solar, wind, and hydro energy production and distribution. Also like their father, they evidently enjoyed procreation and had a lot of children, who also had a lot of children. The business grew and prospered, and the family grew and prospered.

Danielle was the dynasty founder's great-great-great-great-great-granddaughter. At her birth, the family probably expected her either to join the

1

business, or to marry well and extend their wealth, influence, and power. Or both. But the older corporate families that controlled the world's economy considered it quite acceptable for members of their newest generation to sow a few wild oats after university. Whether it was called 'seasoning,' or 'gaining a broader perspective,' it kept the young inheritors' wild and undisciplined behavior out of the corporate halls until they were ready to settle down and get serious about making a few more billion or trillion credits to pass on to the following generation.

That would have been Danielle's path in life had she survived past her first birthday. Not only had Danielle died at an early age, but her parents and her younger siblings, who she never met, had taken an ill-fated airplane ride a few years later, leaving no close relatives.

Since the Kincaid clan was so large, and spread so widely around the world, it was easy to take her identity and create the person she might have become. Through manipulation of various databases, including those inside Kincaid Controls Corporation, plus the planting of fake news stories on various net sites, she came back to life.

⊕⊕⊕

"Danielle! I'm so glad you could make it!" Marian Clark leaned close and we air-kissed each other's cheek. Marian was the kind of effusive, cheerful woman whose speech was always somewhat breathy and excited. She was also the hottest and most exclusive hostess at the top end of Vancouver society. Her dark hair was perfectly coifed, her blue silk dress cost enough to support a middle-class family for a year, and her jewelry was even more lavish than my own.

I'd been in town for over a month, and had finally managed an invitation to one of her soirees. Of course I came. I would have crawled over broken glass to get there. If I could impress Marian and her friends, I'd be in—on the guest list of everyone who was anyone.

She introduced me to Sheila Robertson and Laura Henriquez—women who were also members of Vancouver social royalty—and turned me over to them to take me around and introduce me.

I recorded everything with a device in my bra. That was not the time to miss a name or forget an expression. Any of those people could be useful or harmful to my reasons for being in Vancouver. Not to mention linking a name to some of the jewelry they wore would help later to identify its location. In general, the jewelry was incredible. I tried not to drool, and was glad I hadn't scrimped on my own wardrobe and accessories. Nothing about Marian or her guests could be described as understated.

Marian also was as subtle as a sledgehammer. The purpose of the cocktail party and dinner was to raise funds for Marian's favorite charity, and I was quickly steered toward her secretary, who was collecting the guests' contributions. Cheryl Frind, who had helped me to get the invitation, suggested that ten thousand would be a proper donation. But I was playing a Kincaid, and I didn't plan to take years climbing the social ladder. The fifty thousand I contributed caused the secretary's eyes to widen slightly, and she gave my face a thorough study. I gave her a slight, acknowledging smile, and received an almost imperceptible nod in response. We were on the same page, and that was good.

Cheryl retrieved me from Sheila and Laura and handed me a flute of champagne immediately after the funds changed hands.

"I don't know what you gave, but you impressed a couple of people," Cheryl muttered. "I could see it in their faces."

I smiled at the curvy, short-haired blonde who had become my closest friend in Vancouver. Barely over thirty, she had grown up in one of the city's prominent families and married into another.

"It's only money," I said, taking a sip of the bubbly. "Getting in the good graces of this crowd is worth it."

She gave me a searching look. "That sounded almost like a business comment. You'll damage your party girl reputation if you're not careful."

With a laugh, I said, "Kincaids are given a shot of business with our mothers' teats every morning. If I stumble across an opportunity, why wouldn't I let my family know about it? They didn't send me to university to study art."

"You know, that's part of what I like about you," Cheryl said. "You don't try to pretend you're just a pretty face."

I reached out and caressed her cheek with my fingertips. "You think I'm pretty? I'm flattered. How jealous is your husband?"

Cheryl blushed and looked down at her feet. And though she didn't answer, she didn't draw away from me, either.

"Your reputation is quite mixed." Marian's voice came from behind me. I turned and found her standing quite close. "It seems almost everyone who has met you has an opinion, and few of them agree."

"Do I contradict myself? I contradict myself, then. I am vast. I contain multitudes," I quoted.

"A Kincaid with a computer science degree isn't a

surprise," Marian said, then smiled. "And somehow, I'm not surprised to hear you quote Whitman, either." She nodded at Cheryl. "I've known Cheryl all her life. Her mother was my roommate at university. She said you were more than you appeared."

I laughed. "She lies. She's simply trying to save the men of Vancouver from my predatory ways. I'm just a typical trust-fund baby partying her way around the world and evading my familial responsibilities."

Marian chuckled. "Please. That's a little too much, even for this crowd. Well, what do you think?" she asked, looking around in a way that asked for comment on her house, and probably on the festivities in progress. I realized she was asking because a Kincaid would be familiar with grand houses and luxury.

The mansion was impressive from the outside, nestled in the forest of Stanley Island in the middle of Vancouver Bay. The winds off the ocean kept the air in the city almost breathable, and out in the bay itself, I had been told, I could take off my filter mask without danger.

Inside the house, of course, the air was filtered. Crystal chandeliers—true lead crystal, was my guess— along with hand-painted wallpaper, cast-plaster crown moldings, and other ostentatious but tasteful touches were in keeping with what I estimated to be a twenty thousand square foot neo-Georgian great house. It screamed money. Big money. Huge money.

"It rivals some of the grand houses in Europe," I answered honestly. "It's a little older than you are, though. Your family's or your husband's?"

She laughed. "The house is over a hundred years old, and contrary to some rumors, I am not that old. My family did build it, though, and since my parents didn't have any boys, I ended up with it."

I shook my head. "But I understood your husband didn't marry you for your money. He had his own."

"No, he didn't. Remarkably, sometimes attraction and even love can also have positive business consequences."

"I think every little girl hopes they're that lucky someday," I said.

"You grew up in Ireland, didn't you?" Cheryl asked.

"Yes, I did."

"I haven't spent any time in Ireland or Britain," Cheryl continued, "but here, I think love plays more of a role in marriages than it might there."

Glancing at Marian, I saw a flash of something cross her face, and wondered if she might consider Cheryl as naïve as I did. While Cheryl's marriage might be as serendipitous as Marian's, it had rescued Cheryl's father's business. And Cheryl—stunningly beautiful, intelligent, and genotyped mutation free—was a perfect corporate-wife candidate. I had done a little research on her when she first showed an attraction and willingness to befriend Danielle.

I had done such research on Marian as well. Her marriage created a merged corporate empire that placed it in the Top Fifty—the fifty largest and wealthiest corporations in the world. Their personal wealth ran to triple figures in billions.

"I was noticing some of the art work," I told Marian. "Some truly impressive pieces." As I spoke, I looked directly at a Monet, one of the *Haystacks* series.

"Are you an aficionado?" Marian asked.

"An interested dabbler," I responded. "I would

love to collect someday, but pieces such as that are so wildly expensive. I've decided I need to be one of those people who discover future grand masters. That way I can scoop up their works for a pittance and then revel in the accolades for my astute eye when the world discovers their genius. And, of course, sell a few pieces at a million percent markup."

Marian laughed out loud. "Oh, I am glad I invited you. You'll have to come to lunch sometime, and I'll show you our collection."

"You'll have to excuse me while I faint," I said, laying the back of my hand on my forehead and swaying. "Would begging be considered unseemly?"

She smiled as she reached out and laid her hand on my forearm. "I shall arrange it fairly soon."

Of the one hundred guests, I had met maybe a dozen previously. Two of the men had asked me out, and I'd gone on a date with the unmarried one. He seemed miffed when I declined to invite him up to my room at the end of the evening, and I hadn't heard from him since.

Being smashingly beautiful, I always attracted the notice of men on the prowl, and in this crowd, also the women who swung both ways. I didn't have to do much to attract people to talk with, and soon a group surrounded Cheryl and me.

One man caught my attention. I judged Langston Boyle—tall, dark-haired, and handsome—to be in his upper forties, with a cultured British accent and a devastating way of looking at women. When he spoke to me, I felt as though I was the only woman in the room. From Cheryl's reaction to him, he had the same effect on her. He didn't wear a wedding ring, and his golden tan showed no evidence that he had taken one off.

"So, what brings you to Vancouver, Miss Kincaid?" he asked in a voice that could melt frozen butter at fifty paces.

"I've never been here," I responded, "and friends have told me what a beautiful city it is. I was rather bored, and decided to check it out for myself."

"I hope that you are finding enough excitement that you'll stay for a while," he said, with a slight upturn of one side of his mouth—nice lips—and a twinkle in his eye.

"I've been having fun," I said, "but I could use a little more excitement. What do you do, Mr. Boyle?"

He tried to effect a casual air as he said, "I'm in the art business."

"Oh? Do you own a gallery?" I looked around the room. "I was just admiring Marian's collection."

"Actually, I'm the Director of the Vancouver Art Gallery. Have you been there?"

"Actually, I have." I had spent several days roaming through the halls of the museum, one of the largest in western North America to have survived both flooding and bombing. The museum was built on a peninsula in the center of the downtown area, but the area had become an island. "I love fine art, and I love your collection. I once dreamed of becoming an artist, but when I grew older, I realized that having no talent might make that infeasible."

He laughed. "I'm afraid I suffer from the same problem."

Cheryl drifted away as Langston and I began wandering around the room and staring at the walls together. Unfortunately, when we were called to dinner, I discovered that Marian had seated us rather far apart. My seat was next to Cheryl's, though.

"You two hit it off quite well," she said as the servants served the soup. Robots could do such jobs, but the true upper crust employed human servants.

"You know I love art," I said, "and he's very handsome and charming."

"That he is."

"Married? I didn't see a ring."

"Neither married nor gay," she replied. "One of the top-five eligible bachelors in the city."

"Never married?"

"No."

"Then he has no intention of ever doing so. At least, not until he's over seventy. By then, I'll be too old for him."

She laughed. "He does like women, though. He's a regular in the news nets. I think his hobby is attending events such as this with beautiful women on his arm."

"Who's his escort tonight?"

Cheryl winked at me. "He didn't bring one. He must have heard you were coming."

After dinner, I called for a car, and as I prepared to leave, Langston approached me.

"I would like to see you again," he said. "Perhaps I could give you a private tour of the Gallery."

"Is that anything like asking me up to your flat to see your etchings?" I asked with a laugh. "I would like that, or maybe dinner, or some live music?" I handed him my card. "I haven't decided whether I should get a place of my own, yet, so I'm still roughing it in a hotel. Give me a call."

CHAPTER 2

Inspecting Danielle in the full-length mirror, I let the illusion go and watched the woman in the mirror grow three inches, her hair lighten to yellow-blonde, her face fill out and her cheekbones flatten. Her shoulders broadened, and her body thickened while her breasts shrank a bit, and her hips narrowed. The teal evening gown and diamonds disappeared, leaving a skin-tight black cat suit. It wasn't very sexy, because of the pockets bulging with weapons and tools. Even after twenty years, it still astonished me that I could do that.

The Libby Nelson I'd spent my life seeing in the mirror was a very different—and more comfortable— woman than Danielle Kincaid.

I stripped out of the cat suit as I made my way to the bathroom to take a shower. I really wanted a bath, but the hotel room tub was too short.

After a month in Vancouver, I was finally making some progress. Of four people I hoped to meet at Marian Clark's that evening, I'd managed to connect with three of them—Marian, Langston Boyle, and George Crawford, owner of a large jewelry corporation. Edward Buchanan, my fourth target, had been tied up for most of the evening in what appeared to be a deep discussion with another man I didn't recognize.

Crawford didn't evidence the least bit of interest in me, which I thought was surprising given the jewelry I sported. His wife seemed even less inclined to make my acquaintance. I knew they had a daughter in her early twenties and a son in his late twenties. If I needed to get closer to Crawford, I might have to look into befriending his children.

My presence in Vancouver was at the behest of Myron Chung, an investigator with North American Insurance Corporation, who contacted me at my home in Toronto. I had done some work for NAI in the past. As I took my shower, I replayed Chung's call in my head.

"Miss Nelson, I have some work for you if you have some time."

"How much time are we talking about?" I asked.

"Maybe as much as six months to a year, maybe only a few weeks."

That would mean putting the rest of my business on hold for too long a time. "Mr. Chung, I don't think I can do that. Where is this work?" I figured I might be able to fit it in if it was in Toronto.

"Vancouver," Chung said. Then he mentioned what he was willing to pay. Then he said he'd pay all expenses, with a quarter of a million credits as an up-front deposit.

That's when I said yes. Never let it be said that I couldn't be bought.

My boyfriend threw a fit.

"What do you mean you're going away for six months?" Wil asked, clearly upset.

"That's how long Chung told me it might take. Six months to a year. But who knows? I might figure it all out and be back in a couple of weeks."

"I don't like you being gone so long."

That stopped me cold. Wilbur Wilberforce, Director of Security for the North American Chamber of Commerce and one of the handsomest men alive, had recently moved to Toronto. Our relationship was definitely on the hot and heavy side, as new relationships often are. But we didn't live together, and neither of us had broached the subject of "long term."

Besides, his job required a lot of travel. I started feeling a little itchy, as I usually did when a man got a little too possessive.

"How many days did you spend in Toronto last month?" I asked.

"Why?"

"How many days?"

I could see him counting in his head.

"Uh, six. No, wait, eight. Six days early in the month and then a weekend at the end."

"Uh huh. And how many days did you spend in Vancouver?" Before I had to endure the counting again, I said, "Four. Eight days here, four there. Just switch things around, and we can spend the same amount of time together."

He glanced at my face, then did a double take. Wil was a smart guy, and I was pleased to note that he recognized that the look in my eyes and my cynical half-smile didn't bode well for his end of the discussion.

"Well, I guess we could work something out," he said.

"That's the proper spirit. Come on out and I'll treat you to some seafood."

The items Myron Chung and North American Insurance wanted me to find were two paintings and a dozen or so pieces of jewelry. With a total valuation of close to a billion credits, they had changed ownership in Pittsburg. Through what probably was an oversight, the legal owners hadn't been consulted, and they got upset. They filed a claim with their insurer, and Chung's bosses were willing to pay an outrageous amount of money to try to recover the articles and prevent having to pay the claim.

Rembrandt's *Susanna and the Elders* and Van Gogh's *A Wheatfield with Cypresses* were famous. The jewelry included pieces from the crown jewels of England and France. Those collections had survived the nuclear bombings of London and Paris, but over the centuries, they had been broken up and scattered.

The theft in Pittsburg had been a sloppy, violent job, and three people died. Two of the thugs involved were subsequently captured and executed, but the leader of the heist and the collector who paid for the operation were never identified. The paintings and jewelry disappeared. That had been three years before. When Chung heard rumors that the paintings ended up in Vancouver, he contacted me.

I spent two weeks studying everything Chung could give me, then consulted my father, who often brokered high-end stolen goods.

"I remember the Pittsburg job," Dad said when I visited him. "A rich industrialist married into an old-money family who owned the paintings. He had pretty good security on his mansion, but the crew that pulled the job simply used brute force. Killed two security guards and Mrs. Crabtree. Only took those two paintings and the jewels, although there were plenty of other high-end artworks they could have grabbed."

"Sounds like a commissioned job," I said.

"Exactly. From what I remember, the Crabtrees owned three Van Goghs, all hung on the same wall, but only one was taken. The three together would be worth much more than the total they'd bring individually, which makes me think the people pulling the job weren't pros. They didn't know art. They were shown pictures of what to take, and that's all they took."

"So, what can you tell me about the collectors in Vancouver?"

He grinned. "A lot of very high-end art is disappearing in Vancouver. A couple of pieces you lifted went to a contact there. I got the impression that some very wealthy collectors didn't care where the art came from, and neither did their friends."

"Really?" One of the things that made famous art relatively safe to own was that it was famous. Steal a Rembrandt, and where do you sell it? Collectors of such pieces usually had to hide them away. "You're saying that people are knowingly buying stolen art and displaying it for other people who know it's stolen?"

"That's exactly what I'm saying. They think they're so far above the law and common ethics that they're untouchable." He mentioned several names, one of which was Marian Clark.

Dad gave me the name of his contact in Vancouver. We talked about a strategy for finding the stolen pieces, and he also gave me a list of artworks owned by collectors in Vancouver but desired by collectors elsewhere—just in case I might stumble across one or more of the priceless pieces some evening when I wasn't busy. If all the rich collectors were honest, art thieves would go out of business.

I spent three days and nights creating Danielle Kincaid, kissed Wil goodbye, then took a train to Vancouver. Wil flew all over the continent for his job, but I preferred to avoid the all too frequent airplane crashes due to violent weather. I spent most of the time either reading or studying the international Art

Loss Database to brush up on those artworks that had gone astray at one time or another.

A month later, I was starting to get a good feel for the upper end of Vancouver society. It had always been a rich city, and the devastation of the other large west coast ports had shifted a lot of money north. Although the climate was much warmer than it had been a couple of centuries before, it was still a lot cooler in the summer there than in Toronto. In fact, a lot of the upper crust from Toronto, Chicago, and other eastern cities had summer homes in and around Vancouver.

The Salish Sea area, from Vancouver Island down to Vancouver and south to Seattle and Olympia, had almost completely drowned over the previous two hundred years. A huge earthquake and a tsunami had piled onto the sea-level rise from the melting polar icecaps. Hundreds of new islands had been created, and ocean-going ships could dock as far east as Abbotsford, fifty miles east of Vancouver. Even more than San Francisco, Vancouver had become the western gateway to North America.

Driving over any of the bridges in Vancouver brought a jarring reminder of how much things had changed. The tops of skyscrapers still visible above the surface of the water drew the eyes down to the drowned city below. I had done the obligatory tourist thing of standing on the bridge between Central Island and Stanley Island. The tops of hotels and office buildings looked like man-made islands. Looking down, I could see streets running between the buildings.

⊕⊕⊕

Two nights after Marian Clark's charity fundraiser, I stood outside Sheila Robertson's home, which was right down the road from Marian's. The local society gossip site on the infonet reported that the Robertsons were attending another charity event in San Francisco.

I'd spent most of the previous two days scouting the property. Using my chameleon mutation, I had evaluated the walls surrounding it. Nice little walled estate, approximately forty acres in size, with riding stables, two swimming pools, and a mansion almost as large as the Clark's home. It had very good security, with some of the same top-end equipment I had installed on a couple of homes outside of Toronto.

But the guards had to open the gates when the non-resident staff went home. Blurring my form, I crawled through the opening and then lay next to the driveway while the minibus drove through, and the guards closed the gate again. Half an hour later, with no detectable activity inside the compound, I rose and trotted toward the house.

The Robertsons were rich enough to own a Rembrandt, which they did, and were close to their neighbors, the Clarks. Banking on Dad's intelligence about Marian and the stolen art clique in Vancouver, I figured Sheila and her husband might be a potential market for the paintings. And if not, then the jewelry she had been wearing at Marian's soiree was a tempting target. Besides, I didn't like the woman. How dared she sneer down her nose at a Kincaid?

Some of the windows in the house showed lights. I knew from my research and previous surveillance of the property that the Robertsons employed twenty-two staff, including landscapers, and fifteen security guards on around-the-clock shifts. Twelve of the staff had departed in the minibus. Chances were that other staff had taken the night off with the Robertsons being out of town.

The blueprints for the house showed ten bedrooms in the attic, arrayed around an open space. With the owners gone, I expected that most of the staff still on site would have retreated to their rooms for the evening.

I used a grappling hook and line to climb up to a balcony. The windows behind the balcony were dark. It only took a few seconds to disable the alarm on the door, and I slipped inside.

Creeping through the house, I found a cook still working in the kitchen. A man I took to be the butler sat in a library or study with his feet up on an ottoman, watching a sporting match on a giant screen and drinking brandy or something from a snifter. The room had a few paintings, mainly of hunting scenes in a nineteenth-century style.

Searching through the other rooms on the ground level, I didn't find anything exciting. Climbing back to the second floor, I found a long hall with art decorating the walls. Some of the pieces I could identify, others weren't famous enough that I would have studied them in school.

The ballroom was another story. Rembrandt's *Storm on the Sea of Galilee,* was stolen from a museum long before The Fall, and had surfaced when the Robertsons bought it 'from a private collection' only a few years before my foray into their house. A number of other priceless works hung on the walls, including a Vermeer, a Potter and a Van Loo, along with those of lesser-known artists. Obviously, the Robertsons were partial to Dutch Golden Age artists.

The third floor revealed the family rooms, including his and her bedrooms. In his bedroom, I found a Manet that was on the list of missing stolen paintings I had studied, but no more Rembrandts or Monets.

The safe behind the Manet held some men's jewelry, a few large loose gems, and a few storage chips. I copied the chips using a portable chip cloner, and pocketed a diamond, two rubies, and a very large sapphire. I tucked the Manet under my arm as I left his bedroom. There wasn't a chance he would report it as missing.

Her bedroom had a lot of tapestries and schlock landscapes on the walls. When combined with the pink and green color scheme, the overall impression was of a woman with zero taste. Her safe, however, was worth the trip. Sheila hadn't taken the fantastic diamond necklace she wore at Marian's to San Francisco. I pocketed it along with the matching earrings and bracelet.

It upset me that I had to leave four other paintings and a Rubens bronze, all listed as stolen in the past decade, but there was a limit as to what I could carry.

Exiting the house the same way I had entered, I walked through the gardens to a point opposite the front gate and went over the wall, setting off alarms and lights. Assuming that the guards would focus their attention inside the walls, I slipped into the woods and made my way to my car—a utility van I'd leased with an old identity I often used.

I drove over the bridge into Central Island and downtown, then over the next bridge to a middle-class neighborhood on the mainland. I parked the van in the garage, stashed the painting and all the jewelry, and sent the data from the copied chips to my mother. If there was anything on them that could be turned into money, she'd figure it out. All of that done, I changed clothes and took Danielle's sports car back to my hotel.

CHAPTER 3

Langston Boyle called the following day and asked me out to dinner. I researched the restaurant he suggested, taking a look at the pictures on their infonet site, and created an ensemble that seemed to be appropriate.

The next evening, he picked me up at my hotel, escorting me from the lobby to a waiting limousine.

"I was beginning to wonder if I had been too forward the other night," I said as we drove across town.

With a wrinkled brow, he asked, "Why would you think that?"

"Well, I hadn't heard anything from you, so I thought you were just being polite when you mentioned us seeing each other again."

He chuckled. "Hardly. It's been a busy week. I had meetings with donors, and we're working on our annual fundraiser."

"Oh, really? And when will that be?"

"Three weeks from tomorrow," he said.

"Is that how long I'll have to wait for my personal guided tour?"

"Oh, no, we can do it before then."

I looked at him through my lashes. "Maybe this evening after dinner?"

His surprise was evident.

"I think museums are so romantic," I purred. "Don't you? In the evening, with no one around, and the lights all dimmed? I once took an evening tour of a museum when I was at university. It was very rewarding."

"Well, I think we could work that out. I wasn't aware that your love of art was so deep."

"Art is enhanced by the company with which it is enjoyed," I said. "And I do appreciate deep enjoyment."

I continued to flirt with him throughout a lovely dinner that included huge crab legs. I didn't know if he had anything to do with stolen art, but it would be a surprise if he was totally ignorant of shady dealings in his own city. He was paid well, but my research showed that his consulting side business paid even better. An idea occurred to me.

"Langston, if I were to decide to buy a painting, who would you suggest I contact here in Vancouver to authenticate it?"

"I do that sort of thing," he replied. "I can also refer you to a couple of other people. What are you looking at?"

"Oh, nothing in particular right now, but I heard a rumor that an unusual piece might be coming on the market. I would need to have it authenticated, and get an objective appraisal. I don't think the broker can be trusted to operate in my interests when he's representing the seller."

Of course, there was no such painting. The idea had just popped into my head. But I was willing to bet that my father could supply a stolen painting if I asked him to. Hell, I could even use the Manet.

After dinner, the limo took us to the museum, and Langston used a passcode and retinal scan to get into the building, then an ID card to pass by the guard desk at the entrance. I memorized the passcode. Getting a picture of his retina would be a bit more difficult.

He led me into the main gallery and we strolled

along. Occasionally, I would stop in front of a painting or sculpture, and he would tell me about it. He also pointed out pieces that he either thought I would enjoy or that he thought were particularly interesting. Our tastes didn't always mesh. I didn't appreciate certain abstract paintings as much as he did.

"I've seen all this," I told him, moving closer and placing my hand on his chest. "I was hoping I might get to see some of the non-public areas. Surely you have some special pieces you'd like to show me. Maybe some non-museum pieces you're appraising?"

He cleared his throat and looked a little uncomfortable. I moved closer, pressing my body against his.

Dropping my voice, I said, "All of this is covered by security cameras. Don't you think we could have more fun if we weren't so public?"

"Oh, well, yes. An excellent idea."

For someone so handsome, rich, and sophisticated, Danielle seemed to knock him a little off balance. He led me to a side door, opened it with a passcode, and ushered me inside. I found myself in a maintenance hallway. Most museums and other public buildings had them. The staff running around doing their jobs tended to disrupt the quiet, contemplative atmosphere art lovers prefer.

"Are we going to see some forbidden art?" I asked with a mischievous grin. "Maybe something pornographic that you can't show the school kids?"

Langston laughed. "Is that what you want to see?"

"I want to see all the stuff you hide away. Why would I want to see all the normal stuff when we're here after hours playing naughty?" I leaned against him and gave him a quick kiss on the lips, then turned away.

He took me up a flight of stairs and through a long hallway, then around a corner and up another short flight of stairs. He keyed in his passcode, and we entered a room with paintings sitting on easels rather than hanging on the walls. I counted eight of the paintings, and two small sculptures on a table.

"Are these recent acquisitions?" I asked. "Or are they here for appraisal?"

"Authentication and appraisal," he answered. "As you said, before someone pays a small fortune for an artwork, they want to know it isn't a fake."

Neither the Rembrandt nor the Van Gogh I sought was there, but their theft was three years old. I did recognize a Monet, *The Beach at Trouville*. It had been part of an exhibition at a museum in Belgrade the previous winter and disappeared at the end of the show, a pretty slick heist that made me suspect another chameleon. One of the sculptures looked familiar, but I couldn't place it. When Langston looked away for a moment, I took a picture of it with a small camera hidden in my bracelet.

"So, tell me about them," I said, smiling and throwing my arms around his neck, giving him a more enthusiastic kiss than I had earlier. "Are they worth millions of credits? Are any of them forgeries?"

With his arm around my waist, he led me around to each piece in turn and told me about it. He didn't falter when we came to the Monet, but didn't mention it was considered a stolen piece. He also downplayed its value, telling me he estimated its worth at twenty-five million credits. I knew it had to be worth at least four times that amount.

The sculpture I thought I recognized was an African piece, and I filed away what he told me about it in my memory.

"So, where did these come from?" I asked.

At that point, he turned reticent. "Various collectors or brokers. You understand, my clients and those who are selling the pieces prefer anonymity."

I gave him a sly grin. "Yeah, I understand that. A friend of my father got into some gambling problems and had to sell some art to pay them off."

He looked relieved when I didn't press the issue. Instead, I flowed into his arms.

"Thank you so much. Maybe next time we can view your pornography collection."

He grinned and leaned forward to kiss me. Art wasn't the only thing he knew. I grew a little weak in the knees. His hand slid down my back and over my ass.

"Oh, my! Look at the time! Oh, Langston, I'm so sorry. I have an early tennis date with Cheryl Frind in the morning. I'm afraid I'm going to have to ask you to take me home. You don't mind, do you?"

"No. No, of course not."

"You are such a dear." I separated from him. "You probably think I'm a horrible tease. Please, don't think terrible things about me. I'll make it up to you. I promise." I laid my hand on his cheek and gave him a quick kiss, then turned toward the door.

He came up behind me and put his arms around my waist, pulling me against him and letting me know how aroused he was. He kissed the back of my head and said, "I'll hold you to that promise."

I giggled. "I'll be disappointed if you don't."

When the limo pulled up in front of my hotel, I leaned over and gave Langston a quick kiss on the cheek, then jumped out of the car before either he or his driver could get out. It was raining.

"Thank you so much. I had a wonderful time," I said, then dashed for the hotel.

Inside, I breathed a sigh of relief. I was playing a dangerous game with Langston. I didn't consider myself a prude, but I was probably the least promiscuous woman I knew. At least in my private life. I had seduced men and women in the interests of pulling off a heist or an assassination, but I found it distasteful and used the tactic only when absolutely necessary.

In my private life, Wil and I had never discussed monogamy. I definitely couldn't talk to the top law enforcement officer on the continent about the occasional necessity to sleep with someone in order to steal their assets. That would be much too awkward.

⊕⊕⊕

Ten days after Marian Clark's charity dinner, I arrived at her door promptly at noon. The butler showed me in, and Marian met me in the reception room off the foyer.

"I'm so glad you could come," she gushed, acting as though I was doing her a favor. We both knew it was the other way around.

"I wouldn't have missed it for the world. I've heard so much about your collection. Langston says it's the finest private collection in this part of the world."

"Oh, Langston, is it?" she said with a conspiratorial grin. "Are you and Director Boyle developing a friendship?"

I gave her a raised eyebrow and grinned. "I understand he enjoys friendships with women. I assume I would be the latest in a long line?"

She laughed as she led me to the second floor.

"I'm sure I don't know how long the line is, but Langston does like the ladies, and he's been a bachelor for a very long time."

"That's what Cheryl said."

The room we passed through was decorated in a seventeenth- and eighteenth-century French style with artwork from that era. The baroque and rococo styles went well with the furniture and the tapestry that covered one wall. Her taste was miles above that of Sheila Robertson.

We walked out onto a second-floor terrace. Manicured lawns and colorful gardens spread out before us. The wall of their compound in the near distance separated the estate from the forest beyond. In the other direction, the water of Vancouver Bay was dotted with islands and the hills of the mainland and Vancouver Island in the far distance.

I immediately noticed that while the terrace was open to the outside air, Marian hadn't donned a filter mask. I took a deep breath and filled my lungs with the clean, ocean-scented breeze.

"Oh, my. This is breathtaking. So beautiful."

A genuine smile lit up her face. "We like it. My great grandfather built the house, as well as the bridges linking the island to Central Island and the mainland."

We sat, and two servants served us lunch with a bottle of white wine.

"Are you enjoying your stay in Vancouver?" Marian asked.

"Very much. It's such a pretty place, and the climate is so nice. Even nicer than Ireland. It doesn't rain as much."

"Are you still staying in that hotel?"

"Yes. I did a little bit of looking for a place, but I really haven't put much effort into it," I replied.

She lifted an eyebrow. "Are you thinking of staying much longer?"

"Yes. I would like to. Cheryl is encouraging me to stay, and I must say the social life, the nightlife, and the men are quite appealing."

"Would you be looking for a house, or an apartment?" she asked.

"I should think a house would be too much. I don't want to deal with hiring and training servants or taking care of the grounds."

Her face lit up. "A friend of mine's daughter is going to Europe for two years to study," Marian said. "She has an apartment in a very nice building near the north side of Central Island. It's small, but not cramped. Would you care to take a look at it?"

"Thank you. Yes, I'm interested."

"It's on the ninth floor and faces the water. It's very secure, which would be a bonus, considering what's been going on lately."

I pretended ignorance. "I don't understand. What's been going on?"

"Haven't you heard?" Marian took a deep drink of her wine, squared her shoulders, and leaned back in her chair. "We have a burglar in Vancouver."

With a laugh, I said, "I'd be surprised if you only have one."

"You may laugh if you wish. I'm talking about an uncommon burglar. Since you were here last, no fewer than four of the people you met that night have been robbed."

"You're joking."

"No. Even the Robertsons. You remember Sheila,

don't you? My nearest neighbors. They were robbed when they were out one evening. Guards on duty, servants in the house, and the best security system money can buy. No one heard a thing, but jewelry was taken from a safe."

I wanted to say that the Robertsons' system was far from the best, but held my tongue. More interesting was no mention of the Manet. "That's awful. You don't think it could have been one of the servants, do you? I mean, that would seem to be a more logical conclusion than someone getting in."

"That's the thing. The thief set off the alarm as he was leaving."

"You said four burglaries?"

"Yes, the Robertsons and the Yangs here on Stanley Island, and two more on Central Island. Robbed of their jewelry while they were away." She waved her hand. "I'm having the entire system upgraded. I'm afraid to leave the house. We could be next."

After lunch, she took me for my promised tour. One room was decorated in a nineteenth-century French style with several impressionist works, including two Monets and a Manet. In the next room, two Picassos hung on the wall. It went on. I counted twenty-three paintings by grand masters, along with three Rubens sculptures. The lesser works I didn't bother to count, but I was sure many of them were worth millions.

I paid special attention to five of the pieces. Two I knew were stolen, and the other three I wasn't sure about. None were on the list Chung had given me of missing art insured by North American. But it stretched my credulity to believe that an astute collector such as Marian didn't know the provenance of the works she hung on her walls. Titian's *Venus and Cupid with a lute-player* had been lifted from a museum in Vienna only two years before. Of course, that was at least the fourth time that painting was known to have been stolen over the previous two hundred years. Very popular.

The room that surprised me the most held the paintings I'd teased Langston about at the museum. At least twenty nudes, including the Titian painting, hung on the walls. The only places to sit in the room were three very plush chaise lounges, which invited thoughts about the room, and Marian, which I decided not to explore.

My brief tours with Langston and Marian confirmed my father's intelligence of a healthy trade in stolen artwork in Vancouver. I was surprised at how little concern the participants had about keeping their acquisitions quiet. Either they truly considered me empty-headed, which I couldn't discount, or they didn't care if I knew the paintings were stolen. The number of stolen art pieces I'd seen during my midnight excursions into the homes of Marian's friends backed up that thinking. I was building quite a collection, but so far nothing that Chung wanted.

CHAPTER 4

Checking the Art Loss Database, I verified that five pieces I had seen at Marian's were listed as stolen. In addition to the Manet from the Robertsons', I had identified and appropriated a stolen Rubens, a Pollock, a Warhol, and a Rousseau at some of the houses I'd burglarized in the city. Dad confirmed that an emerald necklace I'd pinched was also on a list of stolen items. The paintings I was trying to recover hadn't turned up, nor had the jewelry or any of the other pieces on North American's list.

I decided to visit the contact my dad had given me. A call to David Abramowitz got me as far as his secretary, who set up an appointment.

The following day, I showed up at his office in an older section of the city. Abramowitz's secretary sported a purple Mohawk, a white plastic skirt that barely covered her ass, and a halter-top that didn't manage to cover her boobs. It was quite a contrast to Abramowitz himself, who was a large man, tall and overweight, about my dad's age—mid-sixties—with a fringe of white hair, dressed in an immaculately tailored suit that was fifty years out of style. His Victorian office furnishings made the suit seem new.

I had debated with myself as to whether I should present myself to the broker as myself—my dad's daughter—as Danielle, or as another persona. I finally decided on keeping to Danielle, but with a minor twist.

"Mr. Abramowitz, thank you so much for agreeing to see me," I said, extending my hand as I entered his office.

"Certainly." He took my hand but eyed me cautiously. "You told my secretary that Jason

Bouchard gave you my name? How do you know Jason?"

"His daughter is my best friend. I've known him since I was a small child."

He nodded and motioned to a chair. "And what is the nature of the business you are interested in?"

"I am acting as an intermediary," I said. "My client is interested in finding two paintings. He has information that they might be in Vancouver."

"Jason said something about missing paintings. Missing Dutch paintings, I believe."

"That's correct."

"Are you aware that people have died for those paintings?"

"Yes, I'm aware of their recent provenance."

Abramowitz shook his head. "Go back to Toronto, or Ireland, or wherever you live, Miss Kincaid. You don't want to get involved."

"I am willing to pay very handsomely for information."

"Go home, Miss Kincaid."

"A quarter of a million for information leading to a recovery. The other three-quarters when I retrieve the items."

That stopped him. As in, he froze and stared at me. I waited.

"What would you expect me to do?" he finally asked.

"I wouldn't expect you to do anything. Simply tell me who has the paintings, or at least who brought the paintings to town and where they went as far as you know."

He bit his lip and stared off into space for a couple

31

of minutes.

"I don't know who has the items you seek. I'm also not sure who commissioned their acquisition. I do know that they were authenticated at the Gallery, but where they went afterward, I have no knowledge."

"Who, in your opinion, would be likely to acquire such works?" I asked. He had verified that Langston was involved with illegal art, but I already knew that.

He squirmed in his chair while I simply sat still and stared at him.

Abramowitz shook his head. "There are too many people to count."

"Oh, come on. Yes, there are a lot of people who would like to lay their hands on them, but these are very high-ticket items. Surely the list of collectors with the funds for such an acquisition is limited."

Patience is a virtue. Eventually, he said, "Clark, Robertson, Aquilini, Audain, Harrison, Fung, Gaglardi."

I took out a payment card with my contact card and slid them across the desk. "That's not what I hoped for, but here's a hundred thousand. If you want more, then get me more."

I stood and walked out of the office, nodding to the purple-haired secretary, who was doing her nails.

⊕⊕⊕

Langston called Wednesday morning and asked me to a play and dinner on Friday night. Figuring I might be able to get some information on him that wasn't on the society or art infonet sites, I called Cheryl and asked her to meet me for lunch.

She suggested one of the two restaurants on Stanley Island, and when I arrived, I saw her seated without a filter mask outside at a table overlooking the ocean.

I shook my head as I sat down. "I've eaten outside occasionally in Ireland, but never in Europe or North America. This is incredible."

Cheryl smiled. "It's my favorite place. It's so amazing to think that people used to breathe unfiltered air even in the cities."

"Well, you wouldn't do that in Toronto or Pittsburg," I said. The waiter came and I ordered. Cheryl already had a bottle of white wine on the table, so he filled my glass. I took a sip, nodded, and winked at him. He smiled and retreated.

"Do you flirt with everyone?" Cheryl asked.

"It's fun. Admit it, you enjoy me flirting with you, and I'm sure our waiter does, too. I can be serious if I want to, but I rarely want to."

"How was your date with Langston Boyle?" she asked, saving me the trouble of guiding the conversation around to him.

"It was fun. He took me on a late-night private tour of the museum. He kisses nice."

"Oh? And will there be a second date?"

"Of course there will. He didn't get what he wanted, so he'll keep coming back until he does."

She laughed.

"What do you know about him?" I asked. "I mean, I can read what's on the net, but where does he come from? What kind of family? Why is he still single?"

The waiter brought our meals. I'd ordered what turned out to be a large salad with crabmeat. He poured more wine, and left us to ourselves.

"Langston's from England, and I get the impression his parents are middle management,"

33

Cheryl said. "He came here for university, went to Europe for graduate school, then came back here and got a job at the museum. Worked his way up and was promoted to Director about ten years ago. Some of the heavyweight donors, such as Marian Clark, supported him."

And I bet I know why, I said to myself.

"Cheryl, you don't seem as though you have much of an interest in art."

She shook her head. "Not really. Neither of my parents care that much about it. I'd far rather go to a concert or a nightclub and listen to music than trudge around through the dusty halls of a museum." She shrugged. "I think art's boring."

She took a sip of her wine, then chuckled. "Langston and I dated for a while about five or six years ago. He couldn't comprehend my attitude toward something he finds so important. It got to where I enjoyed pulling his chain about it. You know, look at a Rembrandt and say, 'That artist wasn't very good, was he? Look at how those peoples' faces are all lumpy.'"

I laughed with her.

"Cheryl, have you ever heard anything about people trading in stolen art?"

With a shrug, she said, "I don't pay attention to such things. If you have enough money, you can buy anything, can't you? Art, boats, horses, women. Everything is for sale."

"That's pretty cynical for a woman who recently told me she married for love," I said.

Her eyes suddenly held a depth I'd never seen there before. "Just because I love Tom, doesn't mean that I don't understand that I was the price to rescue my father's business. Taking a DNA test before you slip the ring on your finger sort of diminishes the romance, but I just ignore things that make me unhappy."

She signaled the waiter and ordered another bottle of wine.

"Speaking of happy," she said after he poured our glasses, "have you been out to Victoria? On the big island?"

"No, I haven't."

"It's beautiful. Tom is going to San Francisco for business in two weeks. Would you like to take our boat over to Victoria for a few days? Just you and me?"

"If a man asked me that..." I let the sentence die.

Cheryl blushed. "You can think anything you like. Do you want to go?"

"Yes, I would enjoy that."

⊕⊕⊕

Wil called on Friday.

"Hey, stranger. It's been a long time. Avoiding Vancouver because I'm here?"

His laugh was so good to hear.

"Actually, I'm going to be flying in there tomorrow. Got any free time, or is your date book filled up?"

"Hmmm, let me see. How long are you going to be here?"

"Fly in Saturday, fly out a week later on Sunday."

"Gee, that's kinda tight. You have to work during the day?"

"Yeah, unfortunately."

"It looks like I may only be able to accommodate you when it's dark. You don't mind if you don't get any sleep, do you?"

"I'm tough. I'll survive."

"Optimist. God, it's good to hear your voice. Where have you been? I'm going to beat you soundly. Bastard. I don't care how busy you are. Call me occasionally."

"Duly noted. Ring up your favorite restaurant and I'll try to make it up to you."

"You bet you will. What time will you be here?"

After talking to Wil, my enthusiasm for my date with Langston took a decided downhill slide. I looked up the play he'd invited me to, and it looked interesting—a new play written only two years before.

When the oceans rose and the bombs fell—a series of events collectively known as The Fall—such pursuits as art, acting, and music took a back seat to survival. Two-thirds of the world's population disappeared before things stabilized, and society in some ways still seemed stuck at the level of the late twentieth and early twenty-first centuries. Science had slowed, but not stopped, but in the realm of aesthetics, humanity hadn't progressed much.

Pleased that I wouldn't have to sit through another production of Shakespeare, I felt a little better.

Langston picked me up, and we stopped by a little place near the theater for an appetizer. The play was very good, thought provoking and emotional. All the lead actor would have had to do was crook his finger and I would have crawled in his pants.

So, I was in a very good mood as we left the theater and headed to dinner.

"Where's your car?" I asked.

"The restaurant is only two blocks away. Do you mind walking? It's a lovely evening," he said.

"Oh, no, I don't mind at all."

I took his arm and we strolled along.

"I've been thinking about you a lot," Langston said.

"And I've been thinking about you."

He suddenly stopped and pulled me into his arms, kissing me long and deep. I hadn't been kissed that well since I said goodbye to Wil in Toronto, and it left me breathless.

I looked around, saw some people staring at us. Some of them were laughing.

"Mr. Boyle. What will people think?"

"I don't care," he said, and kissed me again. I found myself melting into him.

As we proceeded along toward the restaurant, I wondered if that was his standard mode of operation, or if he was truly sincere. If I hadn't been in love with Wil, such behavior, such kisses, would have been a powerful motivator to shed my panties before the end of the night. Actually, Wil's phone call probably saved me from throwing caution to the winds. I sternly told myself to calm down and get my act together.

When the waiter cleared our plates after we'd finished eating, Langston ordered coffee and cognac and asked me, "Would you care to see the dessert menu?"

Since watching Danielle's girlish figure wasn't a concern, of course I wanted dessert. It gave me more time to think about what I was going to do once we left the restaurant. I had set this up on our previous date, thinking that I might want to get inside

Langston's home. That still wasn't a bad idea, but I needed to figure out how to do it without spending time between his sheets.

Sometimes honesty is the best policy. Getting in the limo, I said, "Langston, I have a friend flying in early in the morning." I leaned forward and gave him a quick kiss. "Be a dear, and take me home without making a fuss."

He gave me a long look, then told the driver to go to my hotel.

⊕⊕⊕

The following day, I drove to my safe house, morphed back to my true form and changed clothes. Then I took the van and drove out to the airport to get Wil. He came off the plane, caught me up, spun me around, and kissed me until I thought I would pass out.

At six-feet-four, with video-star looks and dark bronze skin, he stood out almost anywhere he went. Generally, when he gave me that kind of treatment in public, I was glad looks couldn't kill. Many of the women watching us wore poisonous expressions. I didn't care, but I watched my back.

While I showered and got ready to go out to dinner that evening, Wil's voice came from the kitchen. "Is this where you've been staying?"

I had to smile. He was probably looking for something to munch on.

"No," I called. "This is the first time I've used the bed. I have a hotel room downtown."

He came back into the bedroom. "So, any leads on finding Chung's missing art?"

"No, but I have confirmed that Vancouver is a hotbed of stolen high-end artworks. Some of your largest benefactors are in it up to their necks."

He scowled, not liking the idea that the large corporations who paid him to keep the peace might be breaking the law. Most of the national governments dissolved during The Fall, and the Chamber of Commerce took over a lot of their functions. The large corporations funded and ran the Chamber to do those things that individual corporations couldn't do. It also mediated issues between corporations, and oversaw the operations of local police agencies. I once asked Wil if he would be the equivalent of an old-fashioned general, and he said that might be close.

"How large are we talking about?"

"Roger and Marian Clark."

His scowl deepened. "These are the paintings from the Crabtree job in Pittsburg?"

"Yeah, that's what I'm looking for. Can you fasten this necklace for me?"

He did, and planted a kiss on the back of my neck. "A bunch of people died. That seems pretty crude for someone as high up as Clark."

"I didn't say they had Chung's paintings. I said there is a lot of stolen art in this town, and the Clarks are involved. Wil, I've seen stolen artworks in several homes, and also at a museum. When I'm through here, I'll give you a list if you want." I shrugged. "I don't know what you could do about it."

I couldn't imagine the cops or anyone else confronting people as rich as the Clarks.

"I worry about you," he said, trying to take me in his arms.

"Don't. You'll smear my makeup, we'll end up back in bed, and we'll starve. Come on, let's go eat."

In Toronto, I ate a lot of meat—beef, pork,

chicken, and mutton—but very little fish. Certified heavy-metal-and-toxin-free fish, mostly from Hudson Bay, was incredibly expensive. In Vancouver, however, they had an abundance of seafood, mostly from the Bering Straits and the Arctic Ocean, that was far more affordable. I found that I loved it. I took Wil to the fanciest restaurant in town.

"You must be making good money on this job," Wil said as he looked at the menu.

"Expense account," I said. "Besides, this is the first time I've eaten here." I tipped my menu to show him that it didn't have any prices. "We'll see who is the most shocked when I pick up the tab—me or the waiter."

Wil laughed. We decided on a bottle of wine, and gazed out the window at the bay.

"So, how are you going about this investigation?" Wil asked.

I told him about Danielle and the high society parties I regularly attended, mentioning the Art Gallery only in passing.

"Be careful, Libby," he said. "You know as well as anyone how people can disappear when they attract the wrong notice from people at that level."

"I think about it all the time. One of my father's contacts here has warned me of the same thing."

A week later I drove Wil to the airport, thinking the week had been too short. I had an irrational flash that I could just get on the plane and go with him. It passed, but when I got back to Danielle's hotel room that evening, I drank myself to sleep.

⊕⊕⊕

CHAPTER 5

David Abramowitz called while I was in the shower and left a message to call him back. When I tried, no one answered the phone.

Cheryl Frind was coming in twenty minutes to pick me up for our trip to Victoria, so I figured I could call the broker back later. Having gathered my bags, I dragged everything to the lift and went downstairs.

I had spent the previous day shopping. Usually, I simply imagined Danielle's wardrobe, but I figured I should have real clothes if I was to stay in close quarters with Cheryl. I wasn't sure what activities she had in mind, so I over packed and had two suitcases in addition to my handbag.

Passing through the front door of the hotel, I turned right, pulling my bags behind me to get out of people's way.

"Danielle!" Cheryl's voice called from behind me. I stopped and turned toward her. The pop of a bullet splitting the air as it passed me was followed by the sound of it breaking the window next to me.

Reflexes took over. I dived to the ground and rolled toward a waiting car. Another pop sounded above me, and the window shattered. I reached into my handbag for my pistol, but didn't draw it. There were witnesses everywhere, some within a few feet of the broken window.

Looking up, I saw Cheryl standing twenty feet away, frozen in place with her mouth hanging open.

"Get down!" I screamed.

She knelt down, a car parked on the street between her and the direction the bullet had come from. A number of other people also dropped to the sidewalk or otherwise took cover.

A security guard, pistol drawn, rushed toward me. I almost shot him, but held up when I realized he wasn't pointing his pistol at me. He knelt down beside me.

"Are you all right, Miss?"

"Yes. I'm okay."

He looked around wildly, then started to rise. I grabbed his shirt and pulled him back down.

"Stay down, you damned fool! Don't give him a target."

I wanted out of there, and my instinct was to blur my form with my chameleon talent and slink away, but I couldn't do that with all the witnesses. The shooter had been close. With both shots. I had no doubts that if I stuck my head up to look around, he'd blow it off. The guy was a pro.

I lay there until the cops came, and even then, I refused to get up until they provided a shield while they hustled me into the hotel. The shooter could use two different strategies after he missed his shot. He could either get the hell out of there, or he could wait, hoping that I would show myself again. A master sharpshooter wouldn't worry about missing me and hitting a bystander. He wouldn't miss.

Sometime later, I sat in the hotel's lounge with Cheryl and a double shot of whiskey on the rocks. I was having trouble drinking it because my hands were shaking so badly. Partly that was adrenaline reaction, but part was pure, unadulterated, old-fashioned terror. I knew I would never come closer to dying than I had that morning.

"Miss Kincaid?" The man standing there was such a stereotyped homicide cop that I almost laughed.

Fedora, long overcoat, cheap suit.

"Yes."

"I'm Inspector Fenton, Vancouver PD. Do you know why anyone would want to kill you?"

Many reasons, but I wasn't going to tell him about any of them. But in the corporate world—Danielle's family's world—assassinations were quite common.

"I don't know. I'm not involved in my family's business, but I do control a fair number of shares. Someone might benefit if my shares reverted to the corporation. Or maybe someone's wife or girlfriend is jealous." I took a swallow of my drink. "Hell, I don't know."

"You didn't find the shooter?" Cheryl asked.

Fenton shook his head. "We think he was on the roof of the building across the street. By the time we arrived, he was gone."

I doubted Fenton's statement. The angle from the roof would mean the sniper was shooting almost straight down. That would be a very low-percentage shot. My bet was from one of the windows much closer to the ground, and my preference would have been third to fifth floor.

The cops finally went away, and I told Cheryl that I wasn't up for going to Victoria. I tried three more times to call Abramowitz before I decided to drive over there. Unsure if I would be coming back, I took everything of any use with me. Blurring my form, I took the back stairs down to the parking garage. I didn't trust my car and didn't want to take the time to check it thoroughly for trackers or explosives, so I hotwired a rental car and took it.

I rang the bell at Abramowitz's office, knocked on the door, and tried to peer in through the windows.

No answer or sounds from inside. While I could have picked the lock, it would have been rather conspicuous standing on the sidewalk of a busy street in the middle of the day.

That night, I bypassed the alarm system and went in the side door. The neat office I had seen on my previous visit was unrecognizable. Someone had obviously ransacked the place.

The secretary sat at her desk with the wide-eyed, shocked expression that people often showed when they'd been shot in the forehead. Her death was easier than that of Abramowitz. He'd been tortured before having his brains blown out.

The living quarters on the two floors upstairs had also been torn apart. I found a tablet, but it had been wiped. I stuck it in my bag and went back downstairs.

The terminals on both desks showed no connection, and the server was blank. I opened it up and took out the storage chips. Depending on how the intruders had wiped the storage, and what tool they used, there was a possibility I could recover the data.

I decided it would be useless to search the place. A number of expensive paintings hung on the walls, both in the office and upstairs. I found a safe in the upstairs bedroom closet hidden underneath a false panel in the floor. It was very well disguised, but I could feel the electronic keypad lock. Considering the state of the place, I didn't bother trying to find the latch for the panel, I just used a strong knife to pry up the floorboards.

Cracking the safe was easy. The jewelry inside was fabulous. I took it, along with five paintings small enough to carry. Hopefully, the police would write the murders off as part of a robbery.

Driving back to the safe house, I had so many

thoughts swirling around in my mind. I had no doubt that Abramowitz had told his tormentor everything he knew about Danielle Kincaid. Her usefulness was at an end.

If I called my dad or Wil, I knew they would tell me to go back to Toronto and forget about the job. Even Chung might decide to call it off. I was stubborn, but not suicidal. It irked me, though, that I'd put so much time and money into the investigation, and made so much progress.

I unloaded everything at the safe house, then drove the rental car back across the bridge into downtown and abandoned it. The three-hour walk back gave me a lot of time to think.

⊕⊕⊕

I had stashed most of my tools and weapons at the safe house, and my computers were set up there. I checked the storage chips from Abramowitz's server. The tool his murderer had used to wipe the primary chip had not only erased the data, but overwritten it with garbage. But whoever did the job was not a computer professional.

Unknown to most people, almost all computers were built with redundant storage. The secondary chip was intact. I had Abramowitz's books, a history of his inventory and his deals, and a lot of other things, including the secretary's artwork and email communications with her lovers. She was a talented artist, and judging from the emails, an even more talented lover.

I spent the day combing through all his files. It was disappointing to discover that everything appeared to be legal. No records of stolen art or transactions that he hadn't reported to the Chamber or recorded with the international art registry.

45

His bank accounts seemed to have a problem, though. For someone dealing in high-end art, his balances were very low. It took me a couple of hours, but I found the account where he was diverting funds. That account had about twenty million in it, and I syphoned half of it off.

When I decided I'd learned as much as I could from the data, I encrypted it and sent it off to Mom, with instructions to forward it to Dad. He might be interested in Abramowitz's contacts and business arrangements.

I fixed myself a sandwich with the remains of the food Wil had bought, then turned my attention to the tablet I'd found in Abramowitz's upstairs living quarters. Once again, the primary storage chip was blank, but the backup chip was intact. With it, I hit the jackpot, although it took me four hours to break the encryption.

All of Abramowitz's transactions with stolen art, contracts with other brokers and thieves, and the link to the bank account where he held his illegal profits were detailed there. He'd done well for himself, I thought as I looked at the deed for an island in the strait between the mainland and Vancouver Island. The bank account contained almost a hundred million credits. I also discovered he had no heirs. The only beneficiary of his will was Karen Schultz, his adopted granddaughter, whose name matched that of his secretary.

At that point, I was in a position to make far more money from Abramowitz's death than I would make if I fulfilled Chung's contract. On the other hand, I had a lot of information that might help me find the Dutch paintings. Decisions, decisions.

The issue of right and wrong bugged me.

Abramowitz probably died because he tried to help me. His granddaughter was definitely an innocent caught in a bad situation. Not to mention that I was sure the same rich puppet master who ordered his murder had also paid someone to kill me.

With a few keystrokes, I would be a very rich woman thanks to Abramowitz. I felt that I owed him. Besides, the man who had tortured him was a very, very nasty guy. If I could find him, I could make the world a better place with a single bullet.

My growling stomach sent me out of the house to an upscale pizza place a few blocks away. Their advertising said that they used imitation meat, rather than the tasteless soy products of a cheaper place. While I munched on a slice with a very good local beer, I came to a decision. I'd scout out the suspects I found in Abramowitz's files and then decide whether to pursue the paintings.

When I got back to the house, I checked the news. Someone had reported Danielle missing, and together with the attempt on her life the day before, it was all over the news. Considering that she wasn't a real person, I certainly didn't want anyone contacting the real Kincaid organization about her.

I picked up Danielle's phone and called Cheryl.

"Danielle? Where are you? Are you all right?"

"Yeah, I'm fine. I saw my name in the news."

"You disappeared. The cops think you were kidnapped or murdered."

"Not that I noticed. I just didn't feel like sticking around when someone was trying to kill me."

"The police searched your hotel room, and your car is still in the garage."

"A friend of mine sent his plane for me. I didn't

think it was a good idea to advertise where I've gone. Hey, next time I'm in Vancouver, I'll give you a call."

For the police, I made a video call to Inspector Fenton. After I convinced him that I really was alive and speaking freely, he said he'd call off the search and notify the media. About three or four hours later, the stories about Danielle disappeared from the net.

CHAPTER 6

Before the contract with Chung, I hadn't been in Vancouver for several years, and other than my forays out with Wil, I hadn't spent any public time on that trip as Libby. Although I had cover as a contractor to NAI, it went against the grain to work with the police, if I could avoid it.

Reviewing the list of Abramowitz's illicit customers, I narrowed the possible destinations for the Dutch masters. Clark and Robertson would have made my trimmed list, but I hadn't seen the paintings at their houses. Considering how prominently they displayed stolen paintings, I crossed them off the list.

I had been in the houses of two other possibilities when I burgled them and hadn't seen the paintings there, either. At the end, I had three names, plus Langston Boyle. A check of Boyle's bank accounts didn't show the kind of money necessary to purchase a Rembrandt. I found three deposits between one and ten million that coincided with transactions recorded between him and Abramowitz, and I decided they were probably commissions. Boyle was acting as a broker as well as doing authentication.

Boyle might be susceptible to pressure. The other three were not. Dominique Aquilini, Jean Audain, and Gilbert Harrison were all names Abramowitz had given me when I met with him. Old, old Vancouver families with truckloads of money. All three were in their sixties, married to their third wives, with reputations as hard-driving, competitive executives. A perusal of Abramowitz's records showed a number of legitimate and illegitimate art purchases made by each of them, including Dutch artists of the Golden Age.

I downloaded plans of each suspect's main home from the Vancouver Planning Department and began studying them.

⊕⊕⊕

Since I had installed security in museums in the past, I was well aware of their weaknesses. Three days after Abramowitz's murder, I went to the Vancouver Art Gallery, paid the entry fee, and spent the afternoon enjoying the exhibits. Shortly before closing, I went to the ladies' room, picked the lock on the custodian's closet, and settled in to wait. My handbag was full of snacks and other food that didn't need to be cooked.

That night, after the lights were dimmed and the security guards had made their rounds, I went to the door Langston and I went through the night he took me to the museum. I used his passcode to let myself into the maintenance hallways. Making my way to that special room where Langston kept his illicit treasures, I again let myself in.

The room had a desk and chair, and a small couch. I set up two alarms, one in the hall and another on the door, that would broadcast to an earbud, and went to sleep.

I spent the following day reading, checking the news on my phone, and eating some of the food I brought. The day after that was much the same until late in the afternoon. The alarm in the hall went off.

I got up from the couch, turned off the light, and morphed into one of my male personas. Picking up my pistol, I stood next to *The Beach at Trouville*, which I had moved to the desk.

Langston came into the room, turned on the light, and closed the door. He held a padded frame, either bringing a painting with him or planning to take one away. Setting the frame down, he turned and stopped as he saw that the easel where the Monet had rested was empty.

"I've always enjoyed Monet," I said.

Langston whirled around and stared at me. I saw his eyes zero in on the pistol.

"I could never afford one," I continued, "but it didn't occur to me that I didn't have to buy it. I guess you can just steal them."

"Who are you?"

"Does it matter? You're screwed, Mr. Boyle. The director of an internationally known museum brokering stolen art. Tsk, tsk. You of all people should know that stealing from the rich is a no-no. You'll be lucky if they sentence you to a mine on earth. I hear the space colonies are a real bitch."

"How did you get in here?"

"Teleportation, Mr. Boyle. There are a lot of strange mutations."

"What do you want?"

"Ah, a much more intelligent question. I want to know your buyer. In fact, I want to know your buyers for all of your stolen goods."

"Are you crazy? They'll kill me."

"You're assuming that I won't. What did you tell David Abramowitz?"

All the color drained from his face, and he swayed. "I didn't have anything to do with David's death."

"Did Abramowitz ask about some Dutch paintings? He knew that you authenticated them."

"I haven't spoken to David for weeks."

51

He was a lousy liar. I looked at the Monet and then at the frame Boyle had brought. The sizes seemed to match. I motioned with the gun.

"Put the Monet into the travel frame," I said.

Boyle' head swiveled back and forth looking from the painting to the frame.

"You can't take that!" His voice changed from shaky to panicked.

"You're not going to stop me. The only question you should worry about is whether you leave this room alive."

I watched him package the painting and hook a carry strap to it. It wasn't insured by NAI, but I was sure whoever the insurance company was, they would pay to get it back.

As I crossed the room to the door to leave, I said, "You can have the painting back if you tell me where the Rembrandt and the Van Gogh are." He stood mute, breathing heavily and watching me with too-bright eyes.

"Oh, well." I walked up beside him, put the muzzle of my pistol against his head, and shot him in the neck with the jet spray I held in my other hand. The fast-acting paralytic dropped him to the floor in a heap. I didn't want him dead.

Searching through his pockets, I found his phone, opened it, and slipped a tiny chip inside. I was curious who he would call when he woke up in the morning. All indications were that he planned to deliver the Monet that evening. The people expecting him probably wouldn't be happy when Langston didn't show up.

I carried the painting through the maintenance hallways to near the main entrance and let myself out into the public hallways. The security guards stopped me and scanned the package, but it hadn't been chipped as all legitimate acquisitions would be.

"It's my class project," I told them. "I brought it in here just an hour ago to show my professor. Call Dr. Boyle and ask him."

While they called and talked to their superiors, I walked out the door, blurred my image, and essentially disappeared. I stood against a wall and watched people run around looking for me, but they gave up after about forty minutes. Then I walked two blocks, put the painting in my van, morphed back to myself, and went home.

⊕⊕⊕

I was starving. I took a shower, then went out to dinner. On the way home, I picked up some more food I could microwave and some coffee.

Sitting at my kitchen table the following morning, I listened for Boyle to make a phone call. As I enjoyed my second cup of coffee with a microwave quiche, I heard his phone connect.

"Where have you been?" a man's voice said.

"There's a problem," Boyle answered.

"I don't pay for problems. Where is the package?"

Boyle stammered a bit, but finally said, "It's been stolen. A man robbed me last night."

A few moments of silence, then, "That is unfortunate." The man's voice was frosty cold, then he evidently hung up.

I scrambled to get dressed, morphed into Jasmine Keller—a female persona I often used—then drove to the museum and parked across the street. I had always seen Boyle chauffeured in a limo, but I knew he owned a car. I located it in the museum parking lot in his reserved space, and waited for him to come out.

His night on the floor didn't do his suit any favors, so Boyle looked a bit rumpled when he rushed out of the museum and jumped in his car. He carried a long thin black box. I couldn't figure out what he'd been doing in the hour since his phone call, and he hadn't called anyone else.

He drove downtown and into the parking garage under a skyscraper. I sat outside and used my tablet to scan the companies with offices there. The largest was BCR—British Columbia Resources—but none of their executives were on my list. The other possibilities for whom he was visiting were a couple of banks.

From there, he led me off the island and out to the North Shore to a house in an upper-middle class neighborhood. He parked in the garage and let himself in. That surprised me. I had assumed he lived in a fancy apartment building in the downtown area.

I drove past and parked around the corner. Blurring my form, I snuck up to his house and peered in the windows until I saw him in a room that looked like an office. He was pulling things out of a safe and stuffing them in a bag.

From there, he went to another room where he packed a suitcase. Retrieving a cooler from the garage, he filled it with food from the refrigerator. Then he hauled it all to the garage and backed his car out to the street.

I sprinted back to my van and followed him again.

We traveled back toward downtown, but as soon as we crossed the last bridge, he turned right and drove along the waterfront. Turning into a side street toward the water, he used a card or passcode to go through a gate that shut behind him. I parked in a public lot across the street, blurred my form, and followed him.

That involved climbing over a fence and jogging down the street he'd taken. It dead-ended at the water. I checked left and right, but couldn't see his car. With a shrug, I decided to try going left. As I trotted along, I passed docks and boats on my right.

About a hundred yards down the street, I sighted Boyle with the cooler in his hands. He carried it onto a large boat and disappeared. A couple of minutes later, he reappeared and went back to his car. Taking his suitcase out of the trunk, he carried that toward the boat.

Boyle was on the gangplank, and I was drawing near enough to see his face when his head exploded. His body pitched forward into the water, and the suitcase tumbled off on the other side.

Even though I was essentially invisible, I dove for cover out of reflex. I recovered quickly, sticking my head up and looking around for the shooter. As far as I could tell, I was the only witness. I had passed a few other people on my way there, but no one was near us. I scanned the area, waiting for the shooter to show himself. I wouldn't have if I were him. My father had drilled that into me until it was second nature to slink away from a kill, whether people could see me or not.

My father hadn't trained the assassin. A couple of minutes after Boyle was shot, a man stood up on top of a two-story building near where I had parked my car. I estimated the distance at close to three hundred yards. That had been a hell of a shot.

I pulled a pair of small binoculars from my bag and zeroed in on his face. I memorized it, sure that I was looking at the man who had tried to kill Danielle. Who had tried to kill me. If I had a rifle with me, I would have taken him out right then and there, but I only had my pistol. A three hundred yard shot with a pistol wasn't even close to realistic. I watched as he packed up and left, carrying a briefcase that contained his rifle.

Knowing I had no chance to catch him, I dashed for the boat. I had to pick my way over part of the gangplank carefully to avoid stepping in the contents of Boyle's head. The police would be there at some point, and I didn't want them thinking anyone had been on the boat after the murder. I noted Boyle's body floating in the water, and then saw the suitcase, which appeared to be sinking.

I jumped down into the boat. Scooping up the bag Boyle had filled from his safe and slinging the strap over my shoulder, I headed for the stairs going below the deck. A quick search revealed two cabins, a galley, and a bathroom. Vaguely, I remembered that boat people called that the head.

I opened every door and drawer but didn't see anything of interest. I pulled out a drawer under the bed in the second cabin and stopped. The two cabins were identical, but that drawer was shallower than under the other bed. Pulling it all the way out, I shined a flashlight into the space and saw a long black box against the wall. It was out of my reach, but I remembered a funny little pole with a hook I'd found in the closet. I grabbed it and hooked the box, pulling it out onto the floor. It was heavy, as was the bag I'd picked up.

The drawer slid back into place and I stood, trying to think where I should look next. That's when I heard footsteps on the gangplank.

A quick look around confirmed that I was trapped. I stepped up onto the bed and backed into the darkest corner of the cabin while I drew my pistol. Whoever it was repeated my search of the other cabin while I hunched down trying to muffle the sound of my breathing.

Then the assassin who shot Boyle appeared in the doorway of the cabin where I hid. I shot him, and he stumbled backward out into the hall, but I didn't hear him fall. I waited, listening for any sound. A scuffling noise was followed by the sound of footsteps going away.

I cautiously crawled off the bed and crept to the doorway. The hall was empty, and I followed a blood trail up the stairs. Peeking out of the hatch, I saw a man going down the gangplank at a stumbling run with one arm hanging awkwardly at his side. I snapped off a shot at him. He jerked but kept going and ducked behind Boyle's car.

My urge was to jump up and follow, but my quarry was a very dangerous man. Following him, even with my image blurred, would put me in the open. When I moved, someone paying close attention could see me.

Instead, I crept across the deck, using as much cover as I could. The sound of a car starting, then backing up along the street away from me, told me the shooter was escaping. I fired three shots at the car, and one hit the windshield, but he kept going. When he reached the cross street, his car screeched to halt, and with squealing tires, drove forward around the corner.

I decided to follow his lead and get out of there. I picked my way across the gangplank. The blood trail got heavier as I followed it, but it didn't noticeably increase past where I had shot him the second time. He was hurt, and he didn't know what I looked like. I

57

called that a win.

Other than the splash of Boyle's body hitting the water and the noise from the shooter's car, the entire incident had been very quiet. Both of us had silencers on our guns. I passed a couple of people getting ready to take their boat out on the water, but otherwise I didn't see any activity at all as I exited the marina and retrieved my car from the lot across the street.

CHAPTER 7

While I wanted to call my father and talk to him, that wasn't possible. We never discussed business on the phone. Instead, I sent him an encrypted email.

What can you tell me about a shooter, about six-two to six-four, muscular, large round head either bald or shaved, nose broken at least once? Probably in his forties. Very accurate.

Boyle had tried to run. He tried that one phone call, and realized his luck had run out. His boat was easily large enough to take him down to Seattle or San Francisco. I didn't know that much about boats. Maybe he could have taken it to Asia. Whoever he called knew about the boat, had guessed correctly as to what Boyle would do, and taken swift and decisive action.

Curious about what Boyle had tried to take with him, I drove back to my house and hauled the box and the bag inside.

My tablet showed an incoming message, and I saw an email from Dad.

Gavin O'Bannon, thug from Ireland. A favorite of organized crime in Europe. I've heard rumors that he's a mutant. Extraordinary long-range eyesight, extra-fast reflexes, very strong. One of my contacts told me once that he is deformed but you can't see it with his clothes on. Known to have a sadistic streak and enjoys torturing people. I've always avoided doing business with him. Why?

I sent him a reply.

He just took out someone I was following.

Dad responded by telling me to be careful, and I promised that I would. Then I turned my attention to

59

Boyle's treasures.

The bag held papers, including documentation concerning his bank accounts, and a small black book with some interesting encoded entries. The rest of the bag's contents consisted of antique jewelry. I ran a scanner over all of it and verified that none of the pieces had a museum microchip. I wondered if Boyle had siphoned off some of the museum's acquisitions before they were recorded, or if he'd received them as stolen goods. Although I didn't recognize any of the jewelry, I thought they might fit in with the crown jewels NAI had sent me to recover. Most of the pieces Boyle had would be hard to sell except to very specialized collectors, and I couldn't even guess the values.

Turning my attention to the box Boyle had brought out of the museum, I discovered it had an electronic combination lock similar to a safe. I passed my hands over the box and felt a battery inside. That might have deterred some would-be thieves, but it played right into my strengths. Shorting out the lock and opening the box took only a few seconds.

Inside, the box was divided into two spaces, each containing a rolled canvas. I carefully unrolled the first one to find Monet's *Springtime*, a small painting about twenty by twenty-five inches. The other painting was larger, Picasso's *Girl with a Mandolin*, one of the most famous and influential cubist paintings in the world. If Boyle had a legitimate claim to ownership of either of the paintings, then I was a virgin.

The Rembrandt and the Van Gogh were still missing, but I was building quite a collection. I put all the loot away and checked the security system. I briefly wondered what the premiums would be like if I boosted my renter's insurance to cover a quarter billion credits.

I poured myself a shot of whiskey and noted that my hands shook a bit more than I expected. Hell, I'd watched a man die, shot the murderer, and escaped with my life carrying two priceless paintings. Just another routine day. Why should I be shaky?

I followed up the first shot with a second. Then I sat back and tried to figure out what to do next.

My first gambit—the impersonation of a nonexistent heiress—needed to be called off due to personal safety issues. My fallback plan was to let Boyle lead me to the paintings. I had definitely played that one wrong and got Boyle killed.

Time for Elizabeth Nelson, Insurance Investigator, to step into the picture.

I used my computer to convert my voice into a man's and called Inspector Fenton. When he answered, I said, "Langston Boyle was killed at his boat this afternoon by a man named Gavin O'Bannon. He took a bullet doing it." Then I hung up, changed clothes, and drove down to the marina.

The cops had the road into the marina closed off, so I again parked in the lot across the street. Wearing a dark suit coat, trousers, and a white shirt, I looked the part of a corporate representative when I flashed my identification and talked my way past the cops guarding the entrance road.

Several cop cars, an ambulance, and two crime-scene vans crowded the area leading toward Boyle's boat. As I approached, I was able to see they had fished the body out of the water, and it lay on the side of the pier. They also had found the suitcase. Men in white coveralls crawled all over the boat.

"You can't come down here, Miss," a detective said as he approached me.

"I'm looking for an Inspector Fenton." I showed him my NAI identification.

He didn't look happy. "Wait here," he said and walked off.

A few minutes later Fenton came to where I stood. I held out my identification again.

"Miss Nelson, I'm Inspector Fenton. Might I ask what you're doing here?"

"North American Insurance is the largest insurer of fine art in North America," I said. "When the director of a museum as prestigious as the Vancouver Art Gallery goes missing, then turns up dead, we're interested."

Fenton looked as though he'd taken a bite of something very sour. "I can understand that, but specifically, how did you manage to come here?"

"Police scanner," I said with a smile and watched his lips pucker even more.

"Why do you say that Boyle was missing?" he asked. "We had no reports of that."

"No one has seen him in two days," I said. "I had an appointment to speak with him. There have been rumors about stolen artworks in Vancouver for some time, and many of those rumors referenced Langston Boyle."

"I see." His puckered lips spread into a frown. "I would think that such thefts would have come to my department's attention."

With a chuckle, I said, "I'm sure the Vancouver Police Department has access to the Art Loss Database. However, I'm not talking about art stolen here in Vancouver."

Fenton didn't like my implication, but he picked up on it readily enough.

"How did he die?" I asked.

With a shake of his head, Fenton said, "We'll have to wait for the autopsy."

I was four or five inches taller than Fenton. Stepping to the side and standing on my tiptoes, I looked at the body twenty yards away.

"Let me rephrase my question. Did he lose half his head after he died, or was that the cause of death?"

The puckered expression was back.

"Inspector, you and I might help each other. I appreciate the job the local police do, and I try to be useful and not get in the way."

"I can appreciate that, Miss Nelson, but..."

I cut him off. "I have a job to do, and so do you. It's so much easier to be friendly about this sort of thing, don't you think? But if I have to go through the Chamber, I will do that. You call my shot, Inspector."

The Chamber of Commerce's security division outranked and supervised the local police. Mostly, they let the locals to their thing, but when the interests of the large corporations were involved, the Chamber often stepped in.

His expression didn't change, but I saw the flash of anger in his eyes. "All right, Miss Nelson. We'll play it your way. As long as you hold up your end of the bargain." He turned to look at the body. "Yes, it looks as though he was shot in the head." Fenton motioned toward the gangplank. "Blood and brains there, and then he fell into the water. The boat has been searched, and we haven't found anything of interest."

"Thank you, Inspector. As to my contribution, I believe you're also investigating the death of another art dealer, a Mr. David Abramowitz. I suspect the two deaths are related."

The expression on his face changed, betraying curious interest. "And why do you suspect that?"

"Both men had a reputation of dealing in stolen art. Both had client lists that included people wealthy enough to afford the kind of art I'm tracking. Both were killed within days of each other."

"What kind of clients are we talking about?"

"The kind of people who live on Stanley Island."

He sucked air through his teeth.

I continued. "I have reliable witnesses who have seen famous stolen artworks displayed in some of the mansions on the island. Now, I'm a realist, as I'm sure you are. The chance of getting a search warrant for any of those houses is less than zero. But there are other ways to recover such assets."

"Do I even want to know?"

I grinned and winked at him. "Some are rather benign. Threats of lawsuits and exposure. Buying a painting back for a fraction of the insured value. NAI and other insurers don't really expect to come out whole on that sort of thing, but they can cut their losses."

"We're talking artwork that costs millions, aren't we?"

I shook my head. "The specific collectables I was sent to recover were insured for almost a billion credits. That's a drop in the bucket compared to what I suspect is hiding in this town." Hell, what I'd seen in the Robertsons' place alone would probably hit a billion. That family had no scruples whatsoever as to buying hot merchandise.

Fenton stared at me with his mouth hanging open.

"So," I said, "do you have any leads as to the killer?"

He cursed.

I grinned. "Just thought I'd ask, since I know that's the first question you'll get from the media."

"Yes, it probably is. We got an anonymous tip about Boyle, and the tipper did mention a name. We haven't had the chance to check it out yet."

I motioned to O'Bannon's blood trail, cordoned off by small orange cones.

"How many times was Boyle shot?"

Fenton squirmed a bit.

"You're holding out on me," I said.

"We have an alert out at all the hospitals and clinics," Fenton finally said. "It looks as though someone else was here."

"Yeah, the shooter," I said. "So that's either from the shooter, or there was a third party. Come on, Fenton, level with me."

He shook his head. "We don't know. The tip we got said the shooter took a bullet."

"And the shooter's name? You said the tipper gave you a name."

"And I said we haven't had a chance to check it out."

The irritation in his voice told me I'd pushed him as far as he was going to go, so I dropped it. "Who do you have at the museum?"

His eyes narrowed. "Why?"

"Well, I'm wondering what's missing over there. I mean, you did send someone over there to secure the place. Right?"

A bit of panic started to creep into his eyes.

"Inspector, if Boyle was involved in shifting stolen art, I doubt he could keep it secret from everyone at the museum. He might have one or more accomplices. Hell, he might have been selling the museum's collection out the back door. If it were me, I'd lock that place down and tell the board of directors to call in the auditors and their insurance company."

Fenton stood staring at me for about a minute, then he whirled away, pulling his phone out of his pocket. He talked for about ten minutes, then hung up and called to the detective I had first spoken to.

"I'm going to meet some of my people at the museum," he told me. "Want to come along?"

I clapped my hand to my chest. "Inspector, you do know the way to a girl's heart. That's the best offer I've had all day."

On the way to the museum, Fenton said, "Please don't take offense, but you do seem young to be in this line of work."

"University degree in computer science with a minor in art history," I replied. "My primary business is security systems. My dad was VP of security at MegaTech, so I've been around security my whole life. My dad and I were installing a system at the Art Institute of Chicago when they had a theft. I helped recover the objects, and NAI liked my style. They occasionally contract me."

MegaTech was one of the fifty largest corporations in the world. Revealing my connection to the upper echelons of the corporate world rarely hurt when I was conducting legitimate business.

I could tell he was sizing me up out of the corner of his eye. I wasn't going to stun the world with my beauty the way Danielle did, but I knew men liked the way I looked. It didn't bother me, and it often made my job easier.

By the time we reached the Gallery, a fairly large contingent of police had secured all the exits, and people were exiting the building in a steady stream.

"I hope all those people leaving are visitors," I said, "and not any of the employees."

Fenton shot me an alarmed look, and started talking on his phone before he finished parking.

"What do you think we should do with the employees?" Fenton asked as we got out of the car.

"Give them each a five-minute interrogation as to where they were when Boyle was killed," I said. "See if you get any interesting reactions when you tell them he's dead and is suspected of art theft. Maybe you'll get lucky, and a guilty conscience or a whistleblower will surface."

Fenton barked a laugh. "Oh, you are young. I remember when I was that optimistic."

Several of the staff were off that day, and the night staff—mostly security and custodial employees—hadn't arrived yet. Half a dozen people who should have been there couldn't be found. The rest were ushered to an auditorium and pulled out for individual interrogation.

Jon Cruikshank, the young detective who sat with Fenton and me in a small room interviewing people, gave me the creeps. It was the way he looked at me, and the way he looked at some of the people we talked with.

Boyle's administrative assistant—a tall, leggy brunette—was the fifth person we interviewed. Her designer suit and five hundred credit shoes seemed a little out of place for an employee at her level.

"Miss Barbara Willis," Fenton started, "I regret to

inform you that Langston Boyle was killed today. Where were you between ten o'clock this morning and three this afternoon?"

She stared at him with a horrified expression on her face, then she burst out crying. The young detective got a puzzled look on his face, and when Fenton looked at him, Cruikshank gave a small shrug.

"Miss Willis," Fenton continued, "we've found some evidence that Director Boyle might be involved in stolen artworks. Would you know anything about that?"

Other than a small hitch in her crying and a quick glance up at Fenton's face, her only reaction was to shake her head. Cruikshank leaned back in his chair and nodded.

Fenton called in a policewoman and said, "Miss Willis, we're going to need to ask you some more questions. The constable will escort you down to our station."

The constable took Willis out. I turned to Fenton.

"I'm pleasantly surprised, Inspector. Very few police agencies in my experience are broadminded enough to employ known mutants."

Cruikshank shot me a look.

"Empath? Not a telepath, I'm sure," I said. "No one is comfortable around telepaths."

"Jon's abilities are invaluable," Fenton said.

"Oh, I'm sure they are."

By the time we'd run through the entire staff, we had sent four people down to Fenton's office for additional questioning. In addition to Willis, Fenton detained Giorgio Wang, the assistant director, Kieran Murphy, an assistant curator, and one of the security guards. When the night staff arrived, we added the sergeant in charge of the night security detail to the list.

Murphy's reaction to news of Boyle's death mirrored that of Barbara Willis.

"What do you think?" I asked Cruikshank as Murphy was led away.

The young detective looked at Fenton, who nodded.

"I think he was doing both of them, but they didn't know about each other," Cruikshank said.

"Do you think both of them knew about his side businesses?" I asked.

"Willis knew for sure. Not as sure about Murphy, but there's something going on there."

"Maybe she suspected something, but wasn't sure what? In other words, she wasn't in on it?"

"Could be. Willis is definitely hiding something."

"Well," Fenton said, rising and heading for the door, "it should be interesting."

As I rose to follow him, Cruikshank said in a low voice, "What are you hiding, Miss Nelson?"

I turned and looked down at him. I was at least six inches taller than he was, not counting my heels. A feeling I couldn't identify told me he was trying to scan me. I had run into empaths in the past, and my own mutation seemed to make me an enigma to them.

"Constable Cruikshank, don't you know it's rude to ask a lady's secrets?"

"I know you're a mutant," he said. "I can read your surface emotions, but that's it. Nothing deeper. But there's something that you're hiding. Something about this case."

I leaned down and whispered, "My agenda and

Inspector Fenton's agenda aren't completely in line with each other."

"I'm shocked, but that's not what I'm talking about. You're a witch, and you know something about these murders that you're not telling us."

He took me by surprise—not so much what he said, but the utter seriousness and certainty with which he said it—and I straightened.

"There are no such things as witches," I blurted.

"Oh, yes there are. I'll be glad to introduce you to a coven, if you like." He regarded me for a few moments, then said, "No, I can't read you. Interesting."

CHAPTER 8

Barbara Willis sat in the interrogation room doing her best to project arrogant upper-class pique. Detective Constable Cruikshank had a different take.

"What do you think, Jon?" Fenton asked as we watched her through a monitor.

"She's about to wet her pants."

Fenton nodded and opened the door. He laid a folder on the table, sat down, and opened the folder. It contained pictures of Boyle. His face was barely recognizable.

"We have evidence that Langston Boyle was involved with dealing stolen art," Fenton said, ignoring the horrified expression on Willis's face. We think he double-crossed someone, and they had him killed. We don't know if they recovered the art or the money they thought he had, but if they didn't, they're going to come looking for it. And anyone they think might have been involved is a potential target."

He looked up from the pictures. "The kind of people we're dealing with don't really care if they get the wrong person." He opened a second folder containing pictures of David Abramowitz and Karen Schultz.

"You worked closely with Langston Boyle," Fenton said. "You were romantically involved with him. Do you think these people will believe you when you say that you don't know where he kept what they're looking for?"

I nudged Cruikshank and pointed. Liquid was dripping off the seat of Willis's chair. From his angle, Fenton wouldn't be able to see it.

"You're damned good, boy," I said.

Willis broke. She told Fenton about the room in the museum where he kept art he was appraising for clients. She told him about the boat. She told him about a cabin on Vancouver Island. She told him about a small black book where he kept his client list and a list of the illegal art he had brokered for them. She mentioned names, specifically Robertson, Clark, Aquilini, Audain, Harrison, and Reagan. The last was the only one I didn't recognize, but I paid attention to it because it was Irish. Someone had brought O'Bannon into Vancouver, and according to Dad, he normally didn't work in North America.

After a constable led her away to book her, I asked Fenton, "So, what are you going to do now? I told you that Boyle's clients were too high up to touch. If she agrees to testify, she'll be a dead woman before she sets foot in a courtroom. As a matter of fact, if you don't secure the recording of that interview, she may be dead by morning."

"Are you insinuating that members of the Vancouver Police Department are unreliable?" His bristling stance would have been funny in other circumstances.

"Are you telling me that no one in this building can be bought?" I countered. "And you called me young and naïve."

"I'll get the recording and its backup," Cruikshank said and took off at a trot down the hall.

Fenton shrugged. "I'm going to talk with Miss Murphy. Maybe her information will be of more use."

⊕⊕⊕

Kieran Murphy stood a foot shorter than I did, a slender, petite, pretty strawberry blonde, with freckles and an Irish accent. Other than being cute as hell, her six-fingered hands drew my attention. She had worked for four years as an assistant curator at the Gallery. While they brought her into the interview room, I checked her bio on the Gallery's infonet site. She took her bachelor's degree in studio art from a university in Ireland, and her master's degree in art history from Cambridge. One of her paintings of the Vancouver harbor in an impressionist style hung in the Gallery. Judging from the picture of it on the infonet, she was pretty good.

"Miss Murphy," Fenton began, "we have information that Director Boyle may have been involved in the transportation and sale of stolen artworks. Would you know anything about that?"

She stared at him for some time, then with a deep sigh said, "I suspected something was going on, I just wasn't sure what. Sometimes a painting or a sculpture would come in, and instead of coming to the curators to evaluate, he would take it as a personal project. A Monet listed on the Art Loss Database came in about a month ago. When I asked him about it last week, he said he knew it was stolen and that he'd returned it to the insurance company."

Another deep sigh and a glance up at the ceiling. "Another painting, about six months ago, he declared a forgery and said he'd turned it over to the police. He's the expert—was the expert, I guess—so it wasn't up to me to challenge him, but I'd seen the painting before, in Europe, and it looked good to me. I asked him what tipped him off, and he gave me a vague story about the canvas not dating to the proper time."

"Did you tell anyone of your suspicions?" Fenton asked.

"Are you kidding? He's Langston Boyle,

internationally acknowledged expert. I'm just a peon. Accusing him of something would be a good way to lose my job and never find another one."

"Were you sleeping with him?"

I could tell she hadn't expected that question. She paled, her eyes turned a little glassy, and fear registered on her face for the first time. Then she blushed and looked down at her hands, twisting them in her lap.

"Yes. A couple of times." Her voice was barely audible.

"I'll tell you what I think," Fenton said, his voice taking on a hard edge. "I think you knew exactly what he was doing, and you helped him. You wanted the money and you were in love with him. You liked the excitement, the feeling that you and he were smarter than everyone else. Isn't that the truth, Miss Murphy?"

"Noooo!" She burst into tears.

I glanced at Jon, who was sitting beside me in the monitoring room, and saw him shaking his head.

"What's the matter?" I asked.

"Fenton's off base," he said. "What he said doesn't resonate at all with her. But she's elated that he's wrong."

"That doesn't make sense. She should be terrified of what he's accusing her of doing."

"Exactly."

"Are the tears real?"

"She's been on the verge of tears since she sat down. She's afraid of something, but Fenton's accusation didn't increase her fear. It actually scaled down a little bit."

"Interesting. Something scares her more than the

police."

He turned to face me. "So it would seem. Are you psychic as well, Miss Nelson?"

"Just really good at reading people," I said. "Out of curiosity, do you find that mutants tend to have a little bit of fear going on all the time? You know, fear of being found out?"

Jon gave a half-shrug. "Most people do. I think being neurotic is a standard human condition. I've found that almost everyone suffers from imposter syndrome. We're all afraid people will find out that we're not as wonderful, smart, competent, or whatever as we purport to be."

Fenton continued to pound on Murphy for another twenty minutes, but didn't make any additional progress. After he returned her to a holding cell, he sat down with Jon and me. Jon told him the same things that he'd told me earlier.

"Willis didn't implicate Murphy, did she?" I asked.

Fenton shook his head.

"Let her go," I said. "But let me escort her out of the building."

Both men scrutinized me.

"I'm going to coopt her. Befriend her. Provide a sympathetic shoulder. Offer to let her help me investigate the true conspiracy, and in doing so, clear her name."

"And if she truly knows nothing?" Fenton asked.

"No harm," I said. "I'll be the one wasting time on a dead end instead of you."

"It's not a dead end," Jon said. "She knows something, but we're asking the wrong questions."

With a shrug, Fenton said, "Have at it."

75

"After you talk with Wang," I said.

⊕⊕⊕

Assistant Director Giorgio Wang was a balding, heavy-set man with jowls that reminded me of a picture I'd seen of a hippopotamus. He was sweating when a constable led him into the interview room, and it only got worse when he sat down.

"Mr. Wang, as I indicated earlier, Langston Boyle has been murdered. We've also found evidence that he was trafficking in stolen art. What do you know about this?"

"Nothing. I'm an honest man, Inspector." Wang's voice trembled, but carried an angry edge. "I basically run the museum. Langston was the outside face, schmoozing with donors and arranging acquisitions. If he was doing something shady, he was doing it away from the Gallery."

Fenton produced pictures of Boyle's private appraisal room. The forensics team confirmed that none of the art in the room had been microchipped. Two of the seven paintings and one small sculpture in the room had turned up on the Art Loss Database.

"Are you familiar with this room, Mr. Wang? I believe that you have the access codes to it."

Wang mopped his face with a soggy handkerchief. "I have the master codes to the entire building, but I never went in there. That was Langston's private domain."

"And you weren't curious? We're in the process of checking your bank accounts, and some of my officers are searching your home as we speak. It would go much easier for you if you tell us the truth."

"I don't know what you're talking about," Wang said, showing increasing agitation. "What right do you have to search my house?"

We heard a knock on the monitoring room door, and when Jon answered it, a constable handed him a folder. Sitting back down, Jon opened it, then let out a low whistle. He showed me the folder and keyed the microphone to the interview room.

"Inspector, our search team found eighteen paintings in Assistant Director Wang's house. Twelve of them are stolen merchandise, and another five are listed as part of the Gallery collection."

Fenton smiled. "As you were saying, Mr. Wang?"

Wang wasn't talking. He grasped at his chest with his right hand, panting as his face screwed up in pain and turned pale. His lips turned blue. Then he fell out of his chair onto the floor and lay there with spasms racking his body.

"Holy shit!" Fenton yelled, jumping from his chair. "Call a doctor!"

Jon began to do that. I leaped from my chair and raced down the hall to the interview room. By the time I got there, Fenton was giving Wang CPR. It didn't appear to be doing any good. A couple of minutes later a couple of medical techs burst in. They took one look at Wang and shook their heads. One of them grabbed Fenton by the shoulder and pulled him away.

"He's dead, Inspector," the tech said.

"Are you sure? Can't you..." Fenton stopped as the man shook his head.

I agreed with the med tech. Wang stared at infinity, and his bowels vacated, stinking up the room.

"I think you should corral the Gallery's board of directors," I said. "I'm not sure who's in charge over there now, but the place is a mess. You're going to have a herd of insurance investigators to deal with once this gets out."

I pulled out my phone and called Myron Chung. NAI paid me to track down stolen merchandise, not to deal with a major crisis at a world-famous museum.

CHAPTER 9

Fenton gave me a head start, so I was leaning against a column in front of police headquarters when Kieran Murphy emerged from the building. I fell in step with her.

"Miss Murphy, I'm Elizabeth Nelson."

"Yes, I remember. I already gave my statement inside."

"A pretty traumatic day. I'm not with the police, Miss Murphy."

She hesitated and turned to look at me, almost stumbling. I reached out and grabbed her upper arm, steadying her, then let her go.

"I'm an insurance investigator. I'm following up some rumors of stolen art passing through Vancouver. I'm in a position to reward anyone who might provide some help with that."

Shaking her head, she started walking again. "I don't know anything about it. I can't help you." She seemed irritated when she thought I was a cop, but I could see her self-assurance slip a bit when I told her my real job.

"Did they tell you that Giorgio Wang died?"

That stopped her completely, and she turned to look up at me. "What? How? When?"

"Heart attack, about an hour ago. The cops searched his house. It was decorated top to bottom with stolen paintings. I also have information that at least two members of the Gallery's board are involved in trafficking stolen art. Everyone with any connection to the museum is going to come under scrutiny. I guarantee it. Good day, Miss Murphy, and good luck."

I pulled out my phone and called for a taxi.

"Wait," Kieran said. "Are you serious?"

Trying to keep a straight face, I said, "Absolutely. As soon as this scandal breaks, I doubt that anyone associated with the Vancouver Art Gallery will ever work in the business again. Of course, that shouldn't affect you as an artist. You should still be able to sell your paintings. It's lucky you have that to fall back on."

The taxi pulled up, and I started toward it.

"Wait!" She came running after me, her straight, waist-length hair flying out behind her. "Suppose I help you. Do you think that would make a difference?"

"It could. Blowups this large have a way of screwing a lot of innocent people. Better to be on the side of the angels from the beginning. I'm on my way to retrieve my car. Can I give you a lift?"

We rode in silence out to the marina. When the taxi dropped us off, Kieran asked, "What were you doing out here?"

I pointed. "Boyle docked his boat over there. That's where he was killed."

She paled slightly. "The police said he was dead, but they didn't say how he died."

"An assassin blew his head off."

Kieran swayed and put her hand on my van to steady herself. I watched her closely, but couldn't figure out whether her reaction was real or acting. It bothered me that I felt I could almost predict her reaction to anything I said. Even so, I was doing no better than Jon Cruikshank at reading her.

"That's why the police are all over this," I continued. "With the discovery of all those paintings at Wang's, this has the makings of a media field day."

"How could I help you?"

"You know the art scene here, the players. You have the password into the Gallery's computers."

"I couldn't do that. That's illegal."

"I'm not asking for anything illegal, but the donor list would be nice. A list of the art the museum has received, where it's stored, and the current inventory. I guarantee those are things the police will have in the next couple of days, but they aren't really going to know what to do with them."

Not that I needed her password to break into the computer system. I had that on my to-do list for that evening, along with eating dinner, watching a vid, and taking a bath.

"Kieran, Wang had five paintings that belong to the Gallery. He had a dozen more listed on Art Loss. God only knows what those people out on Stanley Island are hiding. I'm willing to bet a large portion of what's in the Gallery's inventory database turns up missing."

I opened the van doors and crawled in, asking, "Where do you live?"

"Out by the university. Do you know where that is?"

"Vaguely. You can give me directions. You wouldn't know a good place to get a drink and something to eat on the way, would you? I can't remember when I ate last."

We ended up in a nice little bistro a couple of miles from the University of British Columbia. As we walked in, a painting caught my eye. When I looked closer, I saw it was signed 'K. Murphy', and had a thousand credit price tag on it. Several other paintings on the wall showed the same style. She definitely had been influenced by the impressionist masters.

"Your work?"

"Yes. An ex-boyfriend of mine owns the place."

We sat and ordered from the automenu. The ale was cold and tasty, the food hot and tasty, and the prices weren't too bad for those things without real meat.

"You strike me as someone who's too smart to fall for Boyle's seduction spiel," I said as we ate.

With a wry expression, she asked, "Did you ever meet Langston?"

"A couple of times."

She gave me a look, wide-eyed and incredulous. "He didn't hit on you?"

"Of course he did. I think he'd probably hit on a robot. It was almost automatic."

Kieran shook her head. "It took me a bit of time to figure it out. I think he was a mutant. Pheromones or something. I don't know. But I wasn't interested in him, and when I was away from him, I didn't want any part of him." She hunched her shoulders, as though drawing into herself. "Usually, you know, at work, it wasn't difficult to be professional. But when he wanted me, all he had to do was make a move. It seemed as though my brain fogged, and I dropped my knickers. Even at work." She blushed scarlet. "When it was over, I hated myself."

"Nope," I said, "never got the urge. Maybe because I was investigating him, and I was sure he was dirty, but I kept making excuses and slipping away. It seemed to irritate him."

With a laugh, she said, "I'll bet it did."

After I polished off my soy burger and salad, I ordered another ale and leaned back to study her.

"When you first talked with Inspector Fenton, you said that you had suspicions about the Gallery. What originally made you suspicious?"

She seemed to think for a minute, then said, "I served internships at a museum in France and one in Ireland. New art came in and went straight to the head curator. The curatorial staff had a procedure we went through. You know, to evaluate it and authenticate it. If we bought a piece, the head curator and maybe one of his assistants gave it a thorough appraisal before the money was paid."

Kieran drained her wine and ordered another glass. "That happened here sometimes. Usually, though, especially with really high value or famous works, they came in and no one knew about them ahead of time except Langston. Often, he would spirit them away to his secret room, and then they might or might not reappear. I just thought it was all very odd."

I had thoroughly studied the procedures at the Art Institute of Chicago when I installed a new security system there, and I had to agree with her.

"What surprises me is that no one else seemed to notice," I said.

"Oh, other people noticed, but everyone just minded their own business. I mentioned it once to Daniel, the head curator, and that's what he told me. 'Worry about yourself, Kieran,' is what he said."

"How well do you know Barbara Willis?"

"Langston's bitch? I know her as well as anyone who works there, which is more than I would wish."

I gave her a grin. "Not a fan?"

Kieran shook her head. "Barbara and Giorgio ran the museum on a day-to-day basis, and Barbara was Langston's enforcer. She did all the unpleasant stuff, such as firing people." Kieran ran her hand through her hair, gathering it and pulling it back off her shoulders. "Barbara doesn't have any friends, at least not at work. All she cared about was Langston."

"Do you think she was in love with him?"

"Oh, yes. Obsessed with him. If he told her to walk off a pier, she would have done it." She turned and stared out the window next to us. The sunlight made her hair light up like gold as she played with it. "So, how can I help you? You said you wanted lists from the computer system?"

"Yes. Do you have to be at the Gallery, or can you access the system from home?"

"I can do it from home."

"Good." I didn't think the police were going to let her into the Gallery. "Do you keep up with the art scene?"

She snorted. "Of course. You want to know who's active, right? Who collects, goes to the artists' shows, gallery openings, all that stuff."

"Yes, and the donors. The ones with the money."

I drove her to her place, a small duplex on a street of small duplexes. Judging from the people I saw out walking, the majority of the residents seemed to be students. She logged into the Gallery's system from her computer and printed me out the lists I asked for.

While she worked, I wandered into the second bedroom, which she had turned into a studio. A half-finished painting of a nude woman sat on the easel. Leaning against the wall were a finished portrait of a nude man and a landscape similar to the pictures at the restaurant.

"You do nice work," I said as I came back to the living room where she worked on the computer.

84

"Thank you."

"Which do you enjoy most, the landscapes or the figure studies?"

"I just started doing the nudes," she said. "I haven't painted any people since I was in France. The models are friends of mine. I'm thinking of doing a series of erotic scenes using them. What do you think?"

"They're both very good looking. Are they lovers?"

"Yes, and lovers of mine. We've talked about it. I think there's a market for eroticism. This is such a decadent city."

I thanked her for the lists and said I'd get back in touch. Even though I could have run the same lists myself, having her do it had saved some time. When I hacked into the Gallery's system, I could focus on looking for things Langston and Wang wouldn't want seen, such as the finances. Langston wouldn't have used his own money to buy stolen artworks.

CHAPTER 10

Myron Chung, Loss Control Director for North American Insurance, flew in the next day from Atlanta along with a couple of his assistants. He called me from his hotel, and I went there to meet with him. It took almost two hours to tell him about everything I'd learned in Vancouver, and I gave him a list of the stolen goods I had recovered.

Myron was Oriental, short and thin, around fifty years old, with black hair that formed a ring around his bald head. "Well, there should be a reward for each piece you recovered," he said. "It might take a little while, and each insurance company will pay after they verify each piece."

I nodded. "That's what I expected. Where do you want me to take it all?"

He thought for a moment. "Let me contact a few people. I'll call you when we figure out a secure location."

"Okay. So, what now?"

"I'll be contacting the local Chamber security head and your Inspector Fenton."

I still didn't understand why Myron had come to Vancouver. "I thought that NAI wasn't involved with the Vancouver Gallery."

"We used to be, until about eight years ago. Another firm outbid us for the contract. You can see how well that worked out. NAI conducts annual audits on the facilities we insure. We would have caught the discrepancies."

Myron walked to the window. The view overlooking the harbor was stunning. He stood looking at the scenery, and I waited.

"Obviously the current insurer is done," he finally said without turning around. "Their inattention will harm their reputation, and I don't think their finances can absorb the loss they're going to take. Your report of widespread trafficking in Vancouver makes me wonder what else is going to turn up. We're here to see what falls out and then pick up the pieces."

"No one will ever be able to touch the board members who are involved," I said.

He turned away from the window. "Probably not, but with your help, we can convince them to resign. Hopefully, with the Chamber's help, we can get a board of directors who are trustworthy." He grinned. "We might even get some of their unorthodox acquisitions returned in exchange for not making a public fuss."

After my meeting with Myron, I felt like I needed a break. Cheryl had told me about a place she sometimes went slumming with her sister. I went home and changed clothes, then set out to find The Blues Note.

Compared to what I was used to, the term 'slumming' didn't apply to that bar. The music was pretty good rhythm and blues, but the menu actually listed real meat, fish, and chicken in addition to artificial meat and soy protein.

She also said a lot of mutants hung out there. That was true, but they were upper-middle class mutants. No one too shaggy or weird. A few well-dressed lycans and vampires were sipping twenty-credit cocktails. I tried to envision a brawl, but failed. None of the patrons would have risked their clothes. It sparked me to thinking about how few mutants I had seen in Vancouver.

Wil called that night after I got home.

"What the bloody hell are you mixed up in now?"

"I miss you, too," I responded. "How sweet of you to call." Honey dripped from my voice.

The silence from the other end told me that he was rethinking his approach. Smart man.

I heard a deep sigh. "Can you please tell me what's going on with the Vancouver Gallery of Art?"

"It seems that the director and assistant were art thieves. They died, leaving stacks of stolen paintings and lots of questions behind. As to how they died, I was a witness to both, but not involved with either. Why?" I put some honey back in my voice. "Are you concerned about my safety? That's so sweet."

"I'll be in Vancouver tomorrow evening."

"How wonderful! Will you be staying long?"

"As long as it takes to straighten that mess out."

"Oh, goody. I hope you haven't packed light. Mess is an understatement, Wil. I suppose you know Myron Chung is here as well."

"Yes. He contacted the Chamber in Vancouver, and they contacted me."

"And they asked you to come up?"

"No. But I figure that anything big enough to put you and Chung in the same city will likely require my attention sooner or later. Sooner is probably better."

⊕⊕⊕

I picked Wil up at the airport and took him to dinner. I'd made reservations at a quiet little bistro with a live jazz band. We had privacy to talk in public, which is what I wanted. He was far less likely to yell when we were in public.

We sipped our wine while waiting for our meals, and I brought him up to date. He got pretty agitated

88

when I mentioned getting shot at while masquerading as Danielle.

"Damn it, Libby. You aren't invulnerable, you know."

"I know."

"You don't act like it. You tell me that a sniper came within inches of blowing your head off with all the emotion most women express in talking about a trip to the beauty parlor."

I took a deep breath and studied his face. If we played poker, I'd own him. His face was so expressive, and his emotions, at least when he was around me, so visible. It was endearing, and I knew he'd never be able to lie to me. It almost made me feel a little guilty, but it wasn't my fault that he was so ready to believe people.

"It's over," I said. "It was days ago, and I already had my freak out." I leaned across the table and took his hand. "I am very aware that I came close to dying. Believe me, I don't take that lightly. I considered abandoning this whole thing and telling Myron to shove it."

His face softened. "So, why didn't you?"

"I've put so much work into it, and I hate to leave a job unfinished. So, I ditched the Danielle Kincaid persona. No one here knows Elizabeth Nelson. I introduced myself to the cops as an insurance investigator. I'm playing this one above board." I winked at him. "Mostly. As far as the people who paid the shooter, I'm starting over and hoping I won't draw their attention in the same way."

I pulled his hand to my lips. "And besides, now I have you to watch my back."

The following morning, I drove Wil to Chamber headquarters and dropped him off. My next stop was at Myron's hotel, where he informed me that we had a meeting with Inspector Fenton and Wil at Chamber headquarters.

I was traveling in circles, as per usual. I called Wil.

"Are you going to come down to the lobby and let me in, or do I have to get undressed in front of the guards at the desk?" I hated going through building security. Even though I had a valid permit to carry a gun, having to show the world two pistols, six knives, plus whatever else I might be carrying at the time was so embarrassing. People never seemed to understand about the garrote or the explosives.

He chuckled. "Yes, I'll come down and save everyone the trauma."

The conference room on the twelfth floor overlooked the harbor and the hills beyond the north shore. In addition to the Vancouver cops and local Chamber security, the meeting included Myron and me representing NAI, three people from West Coast Assurance—the insurance company for the Gallery— and five people from the North American Museum Alliance. It was a large room, and it was crowded.

Fenton briefed the gathering on the murders, Wang's death, and the stolen paintings they recovered from Wang's home and Boyle's workroom. When he finished, he turned the meeting over to Wil.

"I guess I'm going to be coordinating this investigation," Wil said. "Inspector Fenton, of course, will continue to be the lead on the murders of Director Boyle and David Abramowitz. Doctor Williams of the Museum Alliance will be conducting an audit of the Gallery's books and inventory."

He took a sip of his coffee and pointedly looked around the room. "There are a lot of interests, and a lot of money involved here. I expect everyone to be cooperative, and play nice with each other. Information will be shared. Anything and everything you learn, find, discover, guess, or suspect will be reported to the Chamber."

I raised my hand. "Does that mean that I should give you the information I've gathered on the richest families in Vancouver?"

"Yes, it does. And I hope that those in this room are professional enough to understand the sensitivity of our situation. My understanding is that billions are potentially involved. Billions and careers. Yours and mine."

Dead silence.

After the meeting, I took him aside. "Are you serious about wanting my suspicions about the cream of society?"

"Of course," Wil said. "But I'm going to control the dissemination of such information very carefully. You and I should discuss the kind of information we will divulge, and what remains eyes-only. Are you free for dinner?"

"Am I free for dinner? Where do you plan to spend the night, Mr. Wilberforce?"

He gave a slight shrug. "I wouldn't presume to tell you what to do or ask for your schedule. Libby, I'm too smart to get in your way, and you aren't working for me." He handed me a key card. "I have an apartment in the building across the street. We can sleep wherever is most convenient. Considering what you have stashed at your place, it might be wise to limit the amount of traffic out there."

That sobered me. I'd been taking extreme

precautions to make sure no one followed me home. "Yeah. Myron is supposed to let me know where I can take all the recovered loot. I'll be glad to be quit of it. Where shall I meet you for dinner?"

⊕⊕⊕

I had discussed Kieran with Myron and Wil separately, and then Wil and I spoke with Fenton. In spite of their skepticism, they gave me leave to use her in our investigation.

I drove out to her place that afternoon, but didn't find her at home. Thinking I might find her at the bistro where she showed her paintings, I dropped by there, but again struck out. I called Fenton.

"Inspector, are any of the Gallery's employees back at work?"

"Huh? Oh, hell no. We have the place shut down. Why?"

"Just wondering. What are they all going to do? Starve?"

"Go on holiday, I imagine. They're all on paid leave."

I changed the subject. "Did you ever get a hit at the hospitals? You said you were checking on that blood trail that led away from Boyle's murder."

"Nothing. We know someone else was there because the blood type was different than Boyle's."

"Whoever it was probably went to a doctor in the mutie zone," I said.

Silence on the other end of the line, then after a long pause, "That would make sense. We don't have many assets inside that community, but I'll send out a feeler."

I hadn't had any reason to interact with the

mutants in Vancouver. Danielle, of course, wouldn't go near the poorer parts of town. I did some research, and found that the city of Vancouver wasn't very friendly toward poor people, especially mutants.

North of the city—way north—the forests had been heavily settled by lycans. Far south of the city, near the old border with the United States, were several large vampire communities heavily involved in ranching. Several slums east of the city had mixed mutant populations.

Vancouver itself, including North and West Vancouver, was a corporate city. Almost the entire population, including any mutants, worked for the corps. From rich executives, through middle management to the people who actually did the work, almost everyone had jobs with benefits. The neighborhood where I rented my safe house was lower corporate class, mostly blue-collar workers, but it had maintained paved streets, neatly kept houses, and all utilities were included in my rent.

I drove east to find the slums. It was a long drive, and I found non-corporate and corporate neighborhoods in patches, with the poorer areas usually near the water. The flooding when the oceans rose had destroyed more than half of the twentieth-century city and pushed the settled parts far from the original city.

Morphing into a vampire persona, I walked through several neighborhoods. Even the slums were better off than the middle-class non-corp mutant areas of Toronto. I checked out a clinic, and couldn't imagine a bleeding criminal walking in and getting patched up. The place was near-corporate quality.

After wasting the afternoon, I decided that I was on the wrong track. O'Bannon had either bled to death, or his client arranged medical care for him. In my experience, assassins were paid to do a job and be discreet about it. The exceptions were those employed by organized crime. The top of the criminal hierarchy employed their own doctors. My dad did say O'Bannon had worked for the mob in Europe.

My phone rang as I drove back into the city.

"Are you on your way?" Wil asked.

It took me a moment to figure out what he was talking about. Checking my chrono, I realized I was already five minutes late to meet him for dinner. I checked the van's GPS.

"Wil, I'm so sorry. I'm at least half an hour away, even if traffic cooperates. Will they hold our reservation?"

"I'll check." He evidently held the phone away from his mouth because for a couple of minutes I could hear people talking in the background. "They have an open table an hour from now," Wil said. "Take your time and drive carefully."

I wondered if that was a snide comment on my driving. Even though it was rush hour, most of the traffic was headed out of the city. I knew the ferries would be full carrying commuters to the myriad islands and across the various inlets.

Wil had chosen a Japanese restaurant. We sat outside on a terrace overlooking the harbor, dining on sushi and tempura.

"Wil, when I was masquerading as Danielle, I was given a tour of the Clark mansion by Marian Clark herself. I saw two hot paintings I immediately recognized, and when I checked later, two others I saw turned out to be stolen, too. There were stolen paintings in the Robertson and Henriquez mansions. All three have family members on the Gallery's board, and Marian Clark holds the chair. In all three cases, the art is displayed in public areas of their homes. They aren't even bashful about it."

"That certainly complicates things," Wil said.

"Do you think we can shame them into giving the paintings back?" I asked. "You know, blackmail them? Myron thinks it's a possibility."

He rolled his eyes. "Do you really think that would work? People at that level are more likely to drop a bomb on you than succumb to pressure."

"Perhaps."

Our table was in a corner near the kitchen, out of the way and out of sight of the main dining room. I didn't see Kieran until she passed the maître d's station on her way out of the restaurant. Her companion was a gray-haired, distinguished-looking gentleman who looked vaguely familiar.

"Wil, see the cute redhead over there?"

"The tiny one with hair down to her butt?"

"Yeah. That's Kieran Murphy, one of the assistant curators at the Gallery."

"Interesting. The man she's with is Michael Reagan, head of the largest criminal organization in Ireland. He has an estate on Vancouver Island near Victoria."

"Really? I think he was at a reception I attended at Marian Clark's. Langston Boyle's assistant, Barbara Willis, said one of his customers for stolen art was a Michael Reagan."

"I wouldn't doubt it. Wasn't Kieran Murphy the girl you wanted to bring into the investigation?"

"Yes. Fenton's empath said he couldn't read her, but both of us felt she was hiding something. How would you get to Reagan's estate?"

"One of three ways. Boat or ferry, seaplane, or helicopter. I imagine he uses a helicopter. It's about an hour by air, three hours by fast boat. My intelligence reports say Reagan's estate is defended like a military base. He's caught up in a turf war with another gang in Ireland and Scotland, so the past few years, he spends most of his time here." Wil eyed me warily. "You aren't thinking of breaking into his place, are you?"

I gave him my best offended glare. "I don't break into places."

He laughed. "What do you call it, then?"

"I don't break things. That's amateurish. I reconnoiter a place thoroughly, then I choose the best time and place to unobtrusively enter. I'm only interested in whether Reagan has any of the art Chung is paying me to find."

"And if he is?"

"Then I have to figure out how to recover it. Wil, the Rembrandt is too damned big to carry it out by myself. I'd need to drive the van into his compound. I don't think that's very likely. But if he has it, then we'll have to figure out how to get it back."

Wil caught my hand. "Be damned careful, Libby. A man like Reagan has a lot of experience in making people disappear." He brought my fingers to his mouth and kissed them. "I love you."

My heart melted. He didn't say it too often, but often enough that I knew he didn't take me for granted.

"I love you, too. Let's get out of here."

CHAPTER 11

Finding the layout of Reagan's estate wasn't easy. Finding the blueprints of the house was harder. Most people didn't ever think about the plans after their house was built, even the super-rich ones. It took me two days to trace the architect to Ireland, and another day to break into the systems of every firm he'd worked for over the previous fifteen years. Finally, I found where he'd archived Reagan's documents.

My next problem was where to print them. My place in Toronto had all the equipment I needed, but in Vancouver, all I had was a laptop and a tiny portable printer. Reading the plans of a seventeen thousand square foot mansion on a laptop screen wasn't particularly useful. My eyes were good, but not that good. I called Wil.

"Wil, do you have a plotter at Chamber headquarters?"

"What is a plotter?"

"A machine that will print full-size blueprints. A four-foot one will do. A six-foot one would be better."

Silence, then, "Blueprints?"

"Yes. I need to do an estimate for a new security system."

"Or to bypass an old security system?"

"Do you have one or not?"

Big sigh. "I'll check and call you back."

Twenty minutes later. "No, we don't have a plotter. My tech people suggested that you call an architectural or engineering firm. Or a company that makes it their business to print blueprints."

Right. Such companies keep records of that sort of

thing. After all, you never know when a thief might be printing something they can't prove a legitimate right to possess.

I spent another two hours checking out architectural firms until I found one with a lousy security system and no night watchman. I called Wil again.

"Wil, I have something I need to take care of this evening," I said when he answered the phone. "I probably won't be finished until midnight. If I don't show up, I'm sleeping at my place."

The offices of Moorcroft, Alison and Wheeler were located in a small two-story building a couple of miles east of BC University. When darkness fell, I waited until the last light went out, and shortly thereafter, the last car drove out of the parking lot.

Blueprints took a long time to print. I didn't bother with the plumbing drawings, but the electrical drawings were critical. Out of sixty drawings for Reagan's mansion, I only printed a dozen, but it took until one o'clock in the morning. I took the drawings back to my safe house and fell into bed.

Wil called the following morning, checking to make sure I was all right. I assured him I was, then started studying the drawings. Myron called at mid-morning and gave me an address to deliver the stolen artworks. I told him I'd deliver them that afternoon. Then I went back to studying the plans.

Around noon, my stomach started rumbling, so I took a shower, got dressed, and drove into town. On the way, I called Wil and asked him to lunch.

"I spent some time with Inspector Fenton this morning," Wil said as we waited for our meals. "He told me there's been a rash of burglaries at high-end residences over the past couple of months."

"That list wouldn't happen to correspond with the list I gave you of people involved in the illicit art trade?"

"There is a remarkable overlap."

I grinned. "If you would like a look at the art they didn't report in their lists of stolen goods, you can help me take the paintings I've recovered to Chung this afternoon."

That got me one of his patented raised eyebrows.

"It could be very dangerous transporting several million in art," I said. "It would be nice if one of the Chamber's finest could supply a bit of security."

"Am I going to see anything illicit that isn't on a list of items previously stolen?"

I shook my head. "I'm in the art recovery business now days. I do have a few things that I'm not giving Chung, but the most recent owner isn't looking for them." I also kept jewelry separate from paintings. No need to confuse things.

"Oh? And why not?"

"He's dead. I have some paintings that Boyle had in his possession. And no one needs to know that."

Wil stared at me with his mouth open for at least a full minute, then asked, "Is that all you're going to tell me?"

"For right now. I can't find any reports that the paintings were stolen, but I also can't find any information as to where they are supposed to be. They disappeared during The Fall. The chance that Boyle acquired them legally is nil. He didn't have that kind of wealth. There's always the chance that they're forgeries, but I don't think so."

I didn't mention the paintings I'd taken from Abramowitz's home, but their provenance was broken when I stole them. I had checked on them, and he legally owned them, along with the other art he had there.

Wil didn't look happy, but he agreed to help me transport the paintings to the gallery Chung designated. We drove out to my safe house, and I asked him to wait with the van in the driveway.

"I can't come in?"

"No. I don't want you to know where I'm hiding things."

"You don't trust me."

"Of course I don't trust you. You're a cop."

I thought his eyes were going to pop out of his head.

With a smile, I pulled his head toward me and kissed him. "Don't take it personally. You do understand 'need to know', right? It's for your own good. Now be a good boy and wait here until I call you."

The paintings were in a closet in the spare bedroom. The security device I'd installed on the door wouldn't kill anyone with a strong heart, but it would incapacitate anyone in the room if it activated. I disabled it and carried the nine stolen paintings I had liberated from the elite of Vancouver to the garage and opened the garage door.

"Wil," I called. "Can you please back the van into the garage?"

He did so, then got out of the van and looked at the paintings. "I didn't think about the frames," he said.

"I only took what I could carry. It takes time to properly remove a large painting from its frame without damaging it, so, I recovered small, high-value works. I have a list of other stolen works I found. If someone wants to pay me to retrieve them, I can do so, but it's going to cost them, and I don't just mean a recovery fee."

"If you don't mind my asking, what is the standard recovery fee?" he asked.

"One to two percent of the insured value."

"And how much is all this worth?"

"One hundred thirty-two million. When the insurance companies get around to authenticating them, which could take a year or more, I'll make roughly one million three."

I had bought some styrofoam and butcher paper. We loaded the paintings and padded them to keep them from shifting or bouncing around. I called Myron to tell him we were on our way, then got behind the wheel of the van.

Myron had arranged with Feitler's, one of the most prestigious galleries in the city, to store the paintings in their climate-controlled vault. He would then post on the Art Loss infonet site that the art had been recovered, and the legitimate owners and insurance representatives would come and claim the pieces. Normally, the storage would be at a local museum, but the Gallery was under too much suspicion.

We were a block from Feitler's Gallery when a rental truck pulled out of the cross street ahead of me and stopped in the intersection. I slammed on the brakes and glanced quickly in my rearview mirror. Another truck with the same markings was following me.

I jerked the wheel to the left, and the van skidded, sliding into the truck sideways. We hit with a loud crash, and I floored the accelerator. Metal screamed as the van and the truck scraped against each other. Once the van passed beyond the truck, I whipped the wheel to the right, jumped the curb, and fishtailed down the sidewalk.

Wil's pistol firing sounded like an explosion in the close confines of the van. My heart jumped in my chest, and I almost lost control of the vehicle.

"Damn! Get a silencer for that thing. You about scared me to death," I shouted at him while wrestling the van back onto the street. A bullet hit the van, and Wil leaned out of the window and fired again.

"Get back inside and get down, you damned fool!" I screamed. I had already scooted as far down in my seat as I could, while still being able see the road.

More bullets hit the van, and he did as I suggested.

The van fought me, listing to the right. I was pretty sure the right rear tire was flat, and it was making terrible noises as it rubbed against the van's sheet metal. Wil was covered in glass from the shattered window next to him, and his door was caved inward.

"Are you all right?"

"Yeah," he answered. "Probably a little bruised. I'll let you know when the adrenaline wears off."

I could see the gallery on the corner ahead of me, but I didn't know if I should go there. On the other hand, the van wasn't going much farther in any direction.

"I'm going to try to make the corner to the left," I said. "When I stop, get out my door."

He barked a laugh. "Thanks for the suggestion."

We made the corner, and when I hit the brakes, the van lurched to the left, hitting the curb and a sign, and scraping to a stop. I shrugged out of my seat belt, drew my pistol, then opened the door and rolled out onto the sidewalk.

I crawled to the end of the building and peered around the corner. The rental truck still sat in the middle of the street. A man got out on my side, but didn't move toward me. Instead, he turned and helped another man out. The second man limped around the truck while the first man covered him, and they both disappeared.

The rear loading door of the truck opened, but from my angle I couldn't see what was happening there.

A glance behind me confirmed that Wil was out of the van and on his feet.

"Stay here," I said, then blurred my form. I jumped to my feet and raced down the sidewalk toward the truck. Behind me, I heard Wil shout my name, then start cursing.

I passed the truck I had hit and reached the truck that had come up behind me. I stopped in front of it and shot the driver through the windshield. The man sitting on the other side ducked, and I saw his door open.

Half a dozen men stood at the back, helping the injured driver of the first truck into the back of the second truck. I braced my back against the wall of a building, took careful aim, and started firing. I was less than thirty feet away, and they couldn't see me. Three of them fell, and a fourth spun away around the truck away from me, grabbing at his shoulder.

The driver of the first truck huddled on the street, trying to make himself small. I shot him in the leg to make sure he didn't go anywhere, changed clips, and edged farther up the street.

I reached a position where I could see two men lying in the back of the truck, pistols pointed out at the street. Another man crouched behind the truck on the side away from me. Three more were running away. They disappeared into an alley.

"Throw your guns down and come out with your hands up," I shouted.

They couldn't see me, and couldn't locate my voice. I fired and hit the tire next to the man crouched outside the truck. The whole vehicle shifted as the tire deflated.

"Last warning," I called, then shouted louder, "On my mark, fire for effect!"

The bluff worked. All the men threw their pistols out into the street.

"Don't shoot," one of them yelled. "We're coming out."

I backed out of their sight, into the closed doorway of a shop, and unblurred my form, hoping that no one saw. I looked back toward the gallery and saw Wil walking toward me. I could hear sirens, so I assumed help was on the way.

⊕⊕⊕

Wil showing his Chamber identification kept the police from arresting us, and when Fenton arrived half an hour later to confirm our bona fides, they finally relaxed.

Fenton took charge, and allowed Myron to move the paintings from my van into the gallery. A couple of the frames had taken some damage, but the paintings themselves looked all right. The hijackers' trucks were rented using fictitious names, which we all expected.

An ambulance took the wounded man away, and several cops stood guard over the other three I'd captured. I stood watching a paramedic check Wil over. Judging from the bruising that was starting on his right side, he wouldn't be very mobile for several days.

"Four dead, one wounded, and three captured. And you say at least three got away?" Fenton asked me.

"At least. I never did get a complete count. The guy riding shotgun in the second truck isn't here. He's the only one I got a good look at. Sandy blond hair and mustache. I could identify him in a lineup. Then three men ran down that alley, but all I saw was their backs."

Fenton shook his head. "I'm glad you two are on my side. Damned good shooting."

Wil glared at me. I winked at him.

CHAPTER 12

Myron stood in Feitler's storage room surveying the art his assistants had rescued from the van.

"That's quite a haul," he finally said. "A Monet, a Manet, a Holcomb, a Harrill, a Rubens, a Pollock, a Warhol, and a Rousseau. Pretty eclectic. I notice they're all relatively small." He turned to me. "So, am I seeing the tip of the iceberg?"

"Yes. Pieces small enough to carry by myself and that would fit in the van."

He sighed.

"What are we looking at here?" Fenton asked. We all turned to him, and he said, "I mean, the value."

"Each of these paintings is insured for between five hundred thousand and forty million," Myron said. "In total, a lot of money."

Fenton whistled.

"Assuming they're all genuine," Wil said.

I turned to him. "And why would you think otherwise?"

"After we're through here, we'll go over to the museum," Myron said. "The audit is turning up some very interesting things."

The light dawned. "No. Please tell me that Boyle wasn't substituting fakes and selling the originals."

"If you like," Myron said. "I'll tell you Santa Claus is real if it will make you happy."

"Crap. Good fakes?" I asked.

"Damned good." He gave me a strange look. "You look like someone kicked your puppy."

I did feel slightly sick to my stomach. "I can understand stealing a painting. I can even understand

106

someone wanting to hang it on their wall, so they could look at it every morning. I've felt that way about an artwork a few times, and if I can't afford it, I buy a print. But painting a copy and taking the real one away from the world..." I shook my head, not able to put my feelings into words. "It just doesn't sit right."

I thought about the implications of forgeries hanging in a major museum. The art world would be turned upside down for a while. Curators and collectors would have to go through their inventories to verify the paintings they had, and top appraisers would be raking in the money.

"What does that mean for business?" Wil asked.

Myron rubbed the top of his head. "Nothing good. It will depress the value of every painting in the world until things shake out. Everyone will be afraid to buy anything."

⊕⊕⊕

Adrian Martel, Director of Compliance for the North American Museum Alliance, was a totally imposing individual, immaculately attired in a suit that cost a small fortune. He stood four or five inches taller than Wil's six-four, and weighed at least three hundred pounds. I guessed him to be in his fifties, with skin the color of black coffee, a hawks-beak nose, and curly salt-and-pepper hair.

He led us to a large room with two guards stationed at both doors. Sweeping his hand toward a number of paintings leaning against the left-hand wall, he said, "Those twenty are stolen. We found most of them in the storerooms, but two were actually hanging on the damned walls."

Turning to a couple of tables on the other side of the room that held seven paintings, he said, "Those

107

are forgeries we found in the storerooms."

"How much of the inventory have you gone through?" I asked.

"Maybe ten percent. The inventory is a mess. Nothing is where it should be, we can't find pieces that should be here, and we're finding pieces that aren't catalogued." He glared at us. "It's as if things are screwed up on purpose so no one can figure out what's going on. Hell, I found a damned Matisse hanging in the Director's office that isn't catalogued."

The longer he talked the more agitated he became, pacing and gesticulating, his voice growing louder.

"Wonderful," I said. "Myron told us the forgeries are well done."

"Of the seven, four would pass almost anywhere. The others would pass anyone but an expert." He pounded the table with his fist for emphasis, and the paintings all jumped and did a dance.

He was so angry that I didn't risk asking how he knew they were fakes. I figured it was safer to take his word for it. I recognized three of the paintings from seeing pictures of them. That meant they were fairly famous.

"How long do you think it's going to take you to get it all straight?" Myron asked in a calm, quiet voice.

"Until fucking doomsday!" Martel shouted.

"I don't think we can shut the museum down that long," Wil said.

Martel visibly struggled to calm himself. "No, you're probably right," he said through gritted teeth. "I'll call in more resources."

On our way outside, Myron leaned over and asked me in a low voice, "Do you think you could inquire about the forger? I can provide information that might be identifying."

"I can ask, of course."

Myron, Wil and I stood alone on the sidewalk outside the museum. "What I'm interested in," I said, "is who knew I was taking those paintings to you this afternoon? You told me where to take them, and I asked Wil to help me. I didn't talk to anyone else. Who's the leak?"

"I've been rather curious about that myself," Wil said.

Myron looked as unhappy as I felt. "I told Fenton," he said.

"Only Fenton?"

"He had one of his detectives with him."

"What about your people?" Wil asked.

"Well, of course my people knew."

"And the people at the gallery where I took them," I said.

"Yes."

I glanced at Wil. "So, we have a dozen people, plus whoever they told. Too damned many to figure out who tried to get us killed."

Myron rented me another van and took us to pick it up. On our way to Wil's hotel, I said, "My bets are on a paid informant at Feitler's, and at least one paid informant with the police. And I'll bet that the two informants aren't being paid by the same people."

"You have a fairly low opinion of the police," Wil said. His face and tone were sour.

"Experience. If you want honest cops, you need to pay them, and no one ever wants to do that. Society wants the police to be adequate but not truly competent. Too many of us have our little secrets. If you had enough cops, and they were good, smart cops, they'd probably bust a bunch of the wrong people. You know, for things like art forgery and trading in stolen goods."

He chuckled. "Yeah, you're probably right. So, who do you think is paying all of these informants?"

"I'm guessing one or more wealthy collectors have one or more informants at Feitler's Gallery. If I knew about certain rare items ahead of everyone else, I might be able to enhance my collection at the expense of my neighbor. Right?"

Wil chuckled again, but winced when he did it.

"As for the police, I'll bet money that the majority of the top families in the city own a cop. At least one. Hell, if I was a cop, I'd certainly want to get on as many payrolls as I could."

He gave me another sour look.

It became clear at the hotel just how much Wil was hurting. He could barely get out of the car without help, and by the time we reached his room and I stripped him and poured him into a bathtub, the entire right side of his body was black and blue. I started to nag him about not going to the hospital, then thought about how much I hated hospitals. Instead, I gave him a large splash of brandy and a couple of painkillers.

Room service must have thought I was weird when I ordered thirty pounds of crushed ice and asked for a fresh pot of hot coffee to be delivered every hour. The ice went into the bath water, and the coffee, liberally laced with brandy, went into Wil to keep his core temperature up.

"Do you know what you're doing?" he asked me.

"Am I a bruise expert? Do as I say, or I send you to the hospital and let them put up with you while I get a good night's sleep."

I didn't live a genteel life. When we first started sleeping together, he made a few comments about my bruises. After a while, he stopped. Might as well comment on the sun coming up.

He shut up and let me torture him. I checked on him regularly to make sure he didn't pass out and drown. When I finally hauled him out of the ice bath and put him to bed, he was shivering and slightly blue, so I held him tight against me to warm him up. I told myself that it was part of being in love, but in the back of my mind, something kept whispering that I'd gone insane. As I drifted off to sleep, I wondered if there was a difference.

⊕⊕⊕

I had always been ambidextrous. Some things I normally did with either my left or my right hand, but I could change without much trouble if I needed to. So, I thought it was pretty funny watching Wil try to feed himself breakfast with his left hand. He didn't see the humor.

After making sure he had everything he needed, especially communications, I drove out to my safe house. Firing up my computer and connecting through a pirate server in Belarus, I entered the Chamber of Commerce's network through a backdoor, and hacked into the Vancouver Gallery. I had a legitimate login to the Art Loss Database.

It took about three hours to write a program that would download the data I needed from all three sources into a database on my server in Toronto, and then integrate and analyze it. I set it running, then sat back and realized I was starving. It was the middle of the afternoon, and I hadn't eaten since breakfast.

I took a shower and called my dad.

"Hi, hotshot. What's going on?" his voice was cheery when he answered.

"This isn't public knowledge yet, but the Director and Assistant Director at the Vancouver Art Gallery were dirty."

"You mean the museum?"

"Yeah. The main museum here. They were dealing stolen art, and we've found some forgeries."

"Oh, boy. I knew that town had a hot market for hot art, but I hadn't heard anything about forgeries."

"Martel says the forger is very good."

"Adrian Martel?"

"Yes, do you know him? Anyway, Myron Chung asked if I could try to find a lead to the forger."

"Adrian Martel is the best there is at detecting a forgery. What artists?"

"Mostly impressionists. Cezanne, Renoir, Pissarro, and Degas were the ones I recognized. There was also something more modern, but I didn't know the artist. They've found seven so far."

"I'll check around," he said in a voice that seemed to tail away.

"You have a suspicion."

"Maybe." He hung up.

A call to Kieran reached her voicemail, but I didn't leave a message. I took a shower and stopped by a take-out Japanese café on my way to Wil's hotel.

The remains of multiple room-service meals on multiple trays sat in the hall next to his door. So much for being nice and getting him eel sushi. I never would have bought the stuff for myself. I found him stretched out on a couch, lying on his left side, watching cartoons on the screen. To be fair, he was only half-awake.

I unloaded the carry-out onto the table. "How are you feeling?"

"Sore." It seemed to take an effort for him to talk. A little bit worried, I walked over and studied him. He seemed rather out of it.

"Did you take a painkiller?"

"Doctor came by. Gave me a couple of shots."

"What kind of doctor? Doctor from where?" I looked frantically around, half expecting an assassin to step out of the bathroom or something.

"Chamber. Did you send out an email from my account?"

"Yeah. I told people not to bother you for a couple of days. Said you had an important project to work on."

His eyes opened a little more. "That's a confidential account. How did you get into it?"

I rolled my eyes. "Would you like each of the steps in sequence?"

"You hacked into my private account." It almost sounded as if he was offended.

"The only thing that ever keeps me out of your accounts is respect for your privacy. I didn't read anything while I was there, if that's what you're worried about. Wil, I've had an administrative account on the Chamber's system for years. Hell, their lousy security bothered me so much that I wrote them a new security manual and cleaned a lot of it up. And I did it for free!"

I wandered back to the table and my tempura, grumbling to myself about some people's lack of gratitude. "Do you want any eel sushi? I bought it just for you. Cause if you don't, I'm gonna toss it."

He sat up enough to eat, and I sat beside him, helping him watch cartoons. It was actually kind of romantic, as long as I sat by his left side. The ice bags on his other side didn't invite much closeness.

"Next time," he said, "turn to the right."

"Huh? Look, I'm really sorry that you got banged up, but that doesn't make any sense. If I was disabled, or the collision involved the steering wheel, they'd have had us."

He sighed.

CHAPTER 13

It took about a week before Wil was fully back in the game, although still moving a little gingerly. I spent my time following Martel around at the Gallery, working through the plans for Reagan's estate, and bugging Inspector Fenton.

Martel's knowledge of artists was encyclopedic. Even if the painting itself was flawless, he pointed out that the angle of the brushstrokes on the forgeries were all the same. Side-by-side with other paintings by the same artist, even I could see they were different.

"That's amazing," I said after comparing the forgery to four other paintings attributed to Monet.

"Yes," Martel said. "In fact, I would go so far as to guess that the forger is a woman. The strokes are lighter, as though the forger's hands didn't weigh as much, and she wasn't as strong as the painter she was copying." He moved to the Degas. "You see the same thing here."

It might have been apparent to him, but in this case, I couldn't see the difference.

I tried calling Kieran several times without any luck, so I asked Fenton about her.

"I left a message for her," he told me, "and she came into the museum the following day. We questioned her for about two hours."

"Was Jon present?"

"Oh, yeah. Detective Cruikshank sat in on the interview. I'm convinced that she didn't have anything to do with Boyle or Wang and their schemes."

I sought out Detective Cruikshank, who said, "I agree with Fenton. I still think she's hiding something, but I don't think it has anything to do with our investigation. Hell, Miss Nelson, almost everyone has something they want to hide."

"Not me," I said with a grin. "I never do anything I'm ashamed of, so I'm an open book."

He shook his head and grinned back. "I'll buy the first part of that sentence, but I have a feeling it would take me forever to untangle all the things you are hiding."

I laughed, but admitted to myself that he always made me uneasy.

When Wil expressed a little bit of cabin fever— "I'm going to go crazy if I have to spend another minute in this damned room!"—I took him out to dinner. I could understand being sick of take-out and room service.

While waiting for our meals, I noticed Kieran sitting at a table across the room. Her long strawberry blonde hair was rather distinctive.

"Wil, that's Kieran Murphy over there, and she's with Michael Reagan again."

His eyebrows went up. "Maybe they're dating," he said after taking a sip of his wine.

"You know men like that don't date."

"Okay, so he's screwing her, if you prefer more graphic terminology."

"That begs the question of why he's taking her to dinner."

"You're screwing me, but you're still taking me out to dinner," Wil said. "I will admit, once you had your way with me, I figured you'd dump me and..." My dinner roll hit him right in the nose. He stared at it sitting on his plate. "That was terribly sophisticated."

"You knew what you were getting into when you

seduced me. Don't give me any crap."

His chuckle was accompanied by a wink.

"Eat fast. Assuming they ever bring our meals," I said.

"Why? What do you have in mind?"

"We're going to follow them." As I spoke, I saw the waiter deliver Kieran and Reagan's dinners.

I signaled to our waitress, and when she came over, I said, "I just got a call, and our babysitter's sick. Can you ask the kitchen if they can hurry our dinner a little bit?"

"Of course," she said. "I'll take care of it."

As she walked away, Wil raised an eyebrow and asked, "Our babysitter?"

"Of course, darling. Don't I look like the kind of corporate wife who lives to pop out babies?"

He stared at me for a minute, then said, "You'd make a disastrous mother."

I felt something warm in my chest, and a smile spread across my face. Picking up my glass, I held it up to him. "That is the sweetest thing you've ever said to me. I'm so glad that we've gotten close enough for you to see the real me."

Wil barked out a laugh, then picked up his glass and clinked it against mine.

Our meals arrived shortly thereafter, and we settled down to eat, keeping an eye on Kieran and Reagan. We finished about the same time, and paid our check as the other two had their desserts and coffee.

While we waited outside in the car, Wil said, "You know they're probably going to take a helicopter out to the island."

"You can order us a helicopter, can't you? Or an aircar?"

"Not a safe passage across the Georgia Straits in an aircar. They aren't very stable, you know. And it isn't easy to be discreet following someone in a helicopter.

"You're such a killjoy. If they do that, we know that she's staying out at his place."

"And?"

With a shrug, I said, "She's sleeping with a crook. Fenton's empath thinks she's hiding something. Whatever's going on, she's dirty."

"I'm sleeping with a crook, and I'm not dirty."

I leaned over and kissed him on the cheek. "Yeah, but you're special."

We watched Kieran and Reagan come out of the restaurant and get into a limousine. It drove away in the direction of Stanley Island, and we followed. As we crossed the bridge, I said, "I have no idea where they're going. Maybe they have an invitation to someone's house.

"There's a small private airport out here," Wil said. "Floatplanes and helicopters."

The limo drove into the airport. We stopped outside the fence.

"Now what?" Wil asked.

"We wait. As long as we're out here, I want a look at how he's traveling back and forth."

"Probably jetcopter, since he's flying at night," Wil said. "The copters are also more stable in bad weather."

I pulled a monocular from my bag.

"Is there a bottom to that thing?" Wil asked.

"What thing?"

"Your purse. I can't believe the amount of junk you carry in that thing."

"It's not a purse, it's just disguised as one. I use it to carry my equipment. Most women carry a ton of makeup and other stuff, but I fill that space with things that are useful."

Sure enough, in about fifteen minutes a helicopter rose into the air and headed out toward the ocean. I snapped pictures with the camera built into the monocular until I was satisfied that I had all the identifying marks and numbers. Then I talked Wil into following the limo back into town, but it went to a garage, and the driver parked it for the night.

"So, what now?" Wil asked.

"We go home. I just wanted to make sure Kieran went out to Reagan's place."

⊕⊕⊕

I spent the following morning studying Reagan's plans and blueprints. I also checked on travel out to Vancouver Island. When I talked to Wil about leaks from various organizations, I never mentioned the Chamber because I knew it would upset him. But Chamber personnel had tried to kill me more than once. I didn't think I could trust the Chamber enough to hitch a helicopter ride.

My dad called around noon.

"What's the scoop?" I asked. "Have you got a forger for me?"

"I'm afraid not, but I do have some information."

"Shoot."

"About five or six years ago, a number of impressionist forgeries surfaced in Europe. A couple

119

of them were identified at reputable museums, and there was a scandal at one of the major auction firms."

"That's why you asked me about the artists. The impressionists are selling for very high prices."

"That they are. Anyway, Adrian Martel was called in to authenticate the paintings, and then everything got very hush-hush. A contact of mine tells me that some of the big boys in the art world got stung, and to save their reputations, the whole thing got swept under the rug."

Disappointment settled in. "So, no one found out who the forger was?"

"If they caught him, no one is talking. I can't even find any rumor or speculation. But the forgeries stopped."

"Thanks, Dad." I hung up and thought very hard. Then I drove down to the Gallery.

I found Martel with his face buried in a computer terminal in the museum's financial offices.

"Mr. Martel?"

He raised his head. It took a few moments for his eyes to focus.

"Ah, Miss Nelson. How can I help you?"

"I'd like to know a little more about some impressionist forgeries in Europe, oh, say about five years ago."

His demeanor immediately became guarded. "I'm not sure exactly what you're referring to. Does Myron know you're here?"

I filed away that Myron Chung had been involved with the cover up.

"No, but I don't clear what I do with Myron. I'm an independent contractor. I was told that you were involved in identifying a number of forgeries. I'm wondering if you suspect the same forger in our current situation."

Martel eyed me warily. "An independent contractor?" He pushed away from the desk and leaned back in his chair. "I don't mean to be offensive, but you strike me as being very young to be providing expertise to someone like Myron Chung."

"Ah, I see. No one told you who I am."

"Not really. I thought you were one of Myron's staff."

I allowed myself a small smile as I anticipated his reaction. "I'm Jason Bouchard's daughter."

He froze for a moment, then burst out laughing. "Of course. I should have known. You look so much like him."

I grinned. I was eight inches taller than my father, although he outweighed me by at least forty or fifty pounds, and he was dark-haired and swarthy with almost hound-dog features where I was blonde and appeared rather Nordic. I actually didn't resemble either of my parents. Mom was a short, redheaded Irish-English beauty with curves that I didn't inherit.

"So," I said, "some impressionist paintings turned up in Europe about five years ago. You were called in, and then all information dries up. I would assume that reputations and valuations were at risk."

With a sigh, he waved me to a chair.

"I assume your father told you of this."

I didn't answer him. Instead, I said, "That's why you pounced on the paintings here so quickly. You recognized the technique."

"A very astute observation, Miss Nelson."

I waited. He waited. Finally, I asked, "Has the painter gotten better? You said these forgeries were practically undetectable."

"Yes, he, or she, has improved considerably. I don't know if I would have identified them if I hadn't seen the technique before. Of course, I had a bit of a head start. I appraised the Degas when it was sold to the Gallery. That's what tipped me off to start looking closer at all the paintings. I knew it wasn't the same work I had seen before. We've dated the canvas they're painted on, and the forgeries are confirmed."

"Have you found any more besides the ones you showed me?" I asked.

"Three. At this point, I have to assume that Boyle and the forger were partners."

⊕⊕⊕

I walked into Wil's office at the Chamber, closed and locked the door behind me. He looked up and said, "Well, hello. I wasn't expecting you."

"Wil, do you have an operative that you absolutely trust? Someone that you know can't be subverted by money?"

He eyed me, then sighed. A lot of people sighed when I asked questions. I thought I should pay attention to whether Wil did that with other people.

"What do you need this operative to do?"

"Actually, I could use two, but one for sure. I want someone to monitor when Reagan is in town. I assume he always uses that jetcopter."

"It is his," Wil said. "I checked. And what would you use the other operative for?"

"Someone to chauffeur me around. If he could swim, it would be even better."

"I wasn't aware you'd forgotten how to drive. But if you need a ride somewhere, I'll be glad to drive you."

I put my hand on my hip and glared at him. After enduring my imagined daggers for a couple of minutes, he gave up.

"Oh, okay. I assume you need someone who isn't overly concerned with the letter of the law. Why someone who can swim?"

"Someone who believes the end justifies the means would be good. It turns out that there aren't any roads to Reagan's estate. It's only accessible by boat."

"You don't trust the local Chamber people, do you?"

"I trust you."

He sighed again. "I can have a couple of people here tonight. Portland office."

"Thanks!" I skipped across the room, plunked myself down in his lap and gave him a big kiss. "What are you doing for lunch?"

"I'm not really hungry."

"That isn't what I asked," I said and kissed him again.

When I left an hour later, I was really hungry.

CHAPTER 14

James Worthington and Karen Lee were a study in contrasts. He was so non-descript as to be unnoticeable, standing right in front of me—brown hair, brown eyes, medium height and build, with absolutely no distinguishing features. Karen, on the other hand, was almost his height, slender and beautiful, with eyes I could have stared into forever, straight, shiny black hair to the middle of her back, and boobs that seemed a little too large for her frame.

"Did Director Wilberforce explain what I need?"

"In vague terms," James said. "He set me up with a job at the private air terminal out on Stanley Island. The Chamber has also parked a jetcopter out there in case you need it. If so, I'll be the pilot."

It was a lot more than I expected. I handed him pictures of Reagan and Kieran, and a picture of Reagan's jetcopter. "I need you to call me and let me know when either or both of them come to the city, and again when they leave."

James grinned. "That's easy enough."

"And me? I was told that I would be your bodyguard."

I choked. I was about five inches taller than Karen, and outweighed her at least fifty pounds. I'd been training in weapons and martial arts since I was four years old.

"That isn't exactly what I need," I said. "More of a chauffeur and a gofer."

She gave me a perky grin. "I can do that, too. But I am a certified marksman with a black belt in Hapkido."

"Let's hope you don't have to use them," I said.

Karen and I took a bus down to the ferry terminal south of the city and booked passage to Victoria. We didn't talk much on the bus, but it was a beautiful day, and we had a chance to get to know each other on the four-hour ferry ride.

"My mother came here from China with her parents when she was three years old," Karen said. "My father's parents came from Korea before he was born. So, I speak barely-passable Mandarin, enough Korean to get by, fluent Spanish, and I have a degree in English."

"So how did you end up working for Chamber Security?"

"They liked my language proficiency and promised I'd get to see the world. So far, I've been stationed in San Francisco, Chicago, Atlanta, and now in Portland. It turns out the world is far smaller than I thought." She laughed.

"I'll put in a bad word for you," I said. "Maybe I can get you exiled to Europe or something."

"Probably get sent to Kansas City or Dallas. Or Siberia. I think I've pissed off the gods."

"That's a very distinct possibility. Are you aware that I asked for an operative with a flexible attitude toward legal and societal norms?"

"Oooo, I'm your girl. Tell me more."

In between ooohing and ahhhing over the islands scattered throughout the channel and the mountains in the distant south, we discussed my plan to break in to Reagan's estate to look for stolen art.

"So, what's in the bag?" Karen asked, toeing the bag on the deck between my feet.

"Equipment. We'll go through everything in case you need to use any of it." I pointed to her bag, almost as large. "Your makeup and nighty for an overnight stay?"

"Of course. Along with some explosives, a sniper rifle, and a raincoat. A girl should be prepared."

We checked into a hotel in Victoria, then rented a car and a boat. It was too late to go out to Reagan's and give me time to scout the place. Karen had been to Victoria before, so she gave me a walking tour. The city was charming, and I could see why people had second homes there.

"I understand that it used to be absolutely incredible," Karen said. "More than half of the original city is underwater now." She pointed toward the harbor. "All of those islands were connected to the main island back then."

I'd always liked Vancouver. But dinner in a lovely little seafood place and then drinks and dancing at a couple of places cemented my love of Victoria. I vowed that I would invest the money I made from that case in a house there. I couldn't wait to show it to Nellie.

At dawn the next morning, Karen steered our boat into the shore a few hundred yards south of the wall surrounding Reagan's estate. Orange buoys stretched out into the harbor for two hundred yards from the walls, setting out a space for his yacht and seaplane to rest undisturbed in front of the mansion.

I hopped out and shouldered my backpack, then I waved to Karen and trekked off into the forest. I carried a GPS tracker that she could use to locate me when I needed retrieval. She planned to wait for me at the town of Duncan, about twelve miles south.

As soon as the trees shielded me from Karen, I blurred my image and headed for the estate. Slowly approaching it, I discovered just how paranoid

Reagan was. The first thing I came across was a chain-link fence with razor wire along the top. Beyond that was an electric trip wire running about a foot from the ground, then the wall a hundred yards beyond. The plans I studied simply showed the outline of a stone or brick wall, but no detail. The wall I saw before me was smooth poured concrete and twenty feet tall. Not a hand or toehold in sight.

I knew from the plans that the compound inside the wall covered about ten acres. I followed the fence all the way around the property, stopping when I saw the water on the other side. I sat down on a log, pulled out my lunch, and ate while I thought. With no knowledge of the number of people inside, or their additional security measures, going over the wall wasn't my first choice. I gazed out at the water and the buoys floating past the boat and the floatplane bobbing in the waves.

My skills didn't include scuba diving, but it looked as though the water route would be the best way into the place.

It started to rain, so I triggered the GPS signal for Karen to come pick me up. There wasn't anything else for me to see from outside.

Karen texted me when she was ten minutes away, and I moved as fast as I could farther up the coast away from Reagan's estate. When I saw our boat turning out of the channel toward the shore, I stepped behind a tree and unblurred my image. I walked down to the beach, tossed my backpack into the boat, pushed it off again, and jumped in.

"Head toward the island out there," I shouted over the noise of the motor, gesturing toward the small island a mile across the channel. She nodded and steered the boat around. Scooting close to her, I brandished my monocular and said, "I want to run back and forth a few times, so I can scout things out from this side.

We drove back and forth a couple of hundred yards from Reagan's shore, travelling a mile in each direction and acting like we were fishing. The boat had fishing poles as part of the equipment when we rented it. Since neither of us had ever fished in our lives, we had a good time pretending to fish, laughing our asses off. At the same time, we took a lot of pictures of Reagan's compound as we passed by.

In addition to the main house, several smaller buildings sat near the compound's walls. We discussed them and decided that was probably where the staff lived.

In mid-afternoon, we watched the jetcopter rise from somewhere behind the mansion. It headed in the direction of Vancouver, and we turned our boat toward Victoria.

⊕⊕⊕

James called me when we were halfway to Victoria.

"The jetcopter you wanted me to monitor just landed."

"Who were the passengers?" I asked.

"Other than the crew, a man that matches the picture of Reagan, a woman who matches Murphy, and four bodyguards."

"Thanks, James. Let me know when they leave."

I turned to Karen. "Those were our targets leaving in the copter. I'm assuming that security will be more relaxed when Reagan is gone. The problem now is how to get inside."

We had dinner in Victoria and brainstormed various ways to get past Reagan's security.

"I could requisition a jetpack from the Chamber," Karen suggested.

"Don't you think he has something in place to keep his enemies from hitting the house with missiles?"

She thought about that, then pulled up some of our pictures on her tablet. "Probably. The damned place is a fortress." Zooming in on some white domes, which probably were three feet in diameter, she said, "Maybe those?" She took a swig of her wine and punched the automenu for another one. "So, what do we do?"

I looked into my glass, shrugged, tossed off the last of my beer, and punched in my own order.

"We keep watching. There has to be a vulnerability we can exploit."

"How long do you usually...uh..."

I grinned. "How long to case the joint? It depends. The idea is to get inside undetected. I'm not in a hurry. We just have to be patient and watch, and figure out people's movements, and find a time when they drop their guard."

"That sounds terribly boring."

I clinked my glass against hers. "It is." I looked out the window at the falling rain. "Probably wet and cold as well."

On our way from the pub to our hotel, I called James. "Would it be possible for someone to stow away on Reagan's helicopter?"

"There is a small cargo hold," he said. "It was designed to hold luggage, and it would be tight, but you might fit. The problem is, a truck just showed up with a load of food, and they loaded it into the copter. I'm told that happens regularly."

"Yeah. They have to have some means of supplying the place. Thanks, James."

"The boat. The yacht," Karen said as I hung up.

"Yeah? What about it?"

"I'll bet the yacht is what they use to haul in supplies. And the staff, the security detail, you know they don't travel back and forth by jetcopter."

It made sense. Reagan's yacht was huge, about a hundred feet long. Boyle's boat was half that size.

"That boat is large enough to sail to Seattle or San Francisco," I said.

"It's large enough to sail to Australia," Karen said.

"And I'll bet it's expensive and takes a lot of preparation and crew, right?"

Karen nodded.

"I wouldn't turn a yacht like that over to a bunch of half-wit thugs. I'll bet there's another boat, a smaller one, that the staff uses."

Before setting out to spend another day spying on Reagan, we made some discreet inquiries and discovered that a smaller boat did exist. One of the workers at a charging station told Karen that the staff at Reagan's came down to Victoria to shop and party a bit on their days off. He pointed out the boat.

"He says it comes in almost every day, with anywhere from six people to a dozen," Karen said when we met at our boat. "That's why we didn't see it yesterday. It was here in town."

We walked over to a hill overlooking where the boat was moored. Through my monocular, I could see two men lounging on the deck of a boat probably a third the size of Reagan's yacht.

"If we can get them off the boat, or distract them somehow, I might be able to find a place to hide," I said as I passed the monocular to Karen.

"How?" she asked as she lowered the monocular after scanning the boat for some time. "There can't be very much of a place to hide. The guy I talked to said the crew will come back with a truckload of food and other stuff."

"I don't know. I have to get on board first."

"But what if you do?" she asked. "What are you going to do at the other end? And how are you going to get out?"

Two days later, Karen strolled down the dock in a skimpy bikini with a cooler full of beer. Reagan's boat was next-to-last of the boats moored there, and we had established that the family who owned the boat on the end were currently on holiday in China. As she approached the boat, the two men on board—different guys from those we'd seen the first time we observed the boat—perked up and catcalled her.

Karen smiled at them, said hello, and stopped to chat. She set the cooler down and, after a couple of minutes, asked them if they would like a beer.

While they rattled beer bottles and ice, I slipped past her in my blurred form and stationed myself near the bow of the boat. I waited, and after a few minutes, the men invited Karen aboard.

When she stepped onto the deck, so did I, using the bobbing she caused to mask my getting aboard. As she settled into a deck chair, I found an equipment locker fore of the cabin. Inside was a large rope, similar to the ropes tying the boat to the dock. It appeared to be a spare, so I pulled it out and dumped it over the side. I had to be very quiet, and had to keep looking for anyone who might look askance at a rope floating through the air by itself.

It took me about ten minutes to quietly feed the heavy rope into the water. I used a lever bar from my pack to break the latch, then I crawled into the locker and pulled the cover closed. It was tight, but not too uncomfortable. I hoped they would pull out that evening. Sometimes they stayed overnight, as they had done the night before. Pulling out my phone, I texted Karen her signal to bail out. Fairly confident that I wouldn't be disturbed, I set an alarm on my chrono for three hours and took a nap.

CHAPTER 15

I said a silent prayer when I heard people come on board. About an hour of scuffling and shouting and banging around, then the engine started. Shortly afterward, the boat started moving.

Once we were out of the harbor and the driver opened up the engine, the other occupants quieted. I risked cracking the lid of the locker a little and let some fresh air into the stuffy space.

The ride from Victoria to Reagan's estate took about forty-five minutes. When the driver slowed the engines, I peeked out and saw the lights on the buoys start blinking, then three of the buoys went dark. The boat glided between them, and though I couldn't see behind us, I was sure the lights went back on.

We passed the yacht, then the seaplane and pulled into the dock. I listened to people coming and going for another hour, then things got quiet again. It was ten-thirty at night by my chrono.

Blurring my image, I slipped out of the locker and onto the deck. Twenty minutes later I was sure that I was alone on board and the dock was deserted. I called Karen and she answered on the first ring.

"Where are you? Are you all right?"

"Sitting on the boat, all alone, taking a look at the house. Most of the lights are out."

"Yeah, at least from where I am. So, you're all right? No problems?"

"Smooth as silk. I'm going to check out the security at the house. I won't call you again until I'm ready to get out."

I kept to the shadows as I made my way to the house. The periphery near the outer wall of the estate was well lit, but only a couple of lights were on at the house itself. It was a sprawling place, two stories high.

The outbuildings showed a little more activity. That was good for me, as it meant the staff were at their homes rather than at the mansion.

I knew from the plans that only two doors existed on the second floor. One led out to a veranda overlooking the front lawn and the water. The other led to a narrow stairway in the back. All the lights were off in the kitchen, so I let myself in there. I was prepared to disable an alarm and pick the lock, but the alarm wasn't on, and the door wasn't locked. Country folk. All the security was in place, but obviously on a day-to-day basis, people didn't bother. Nothing had ever occurred to make the inhabitants security conscious. The focus was all on the outskirts of the property.

Hugging the walls and moving slowly, with my form blurred and wearing night-vision goggles, I knew the chances of me being detected were very low. I moved from room to room, checking out the impressive furniture and art works.

The dining room displayed some of the original impressionist paintings whose copies sat in the Gallery in Vancouver. In what I could only describe as the most stereotypical study-library-mancave I'd ever seen, Rembrandt's *Storm on the Sea of Galilee* proudly held a place of honor. I had to chuckle. Surely the Robertsons had paid a small fortune for their version of the painting, but I wasn't taking any bets as to which was the genuine article. *Susanna and the Elders* hung on the opposite wall.

A sideboard held an enviable set of lead crystal decanters and glasses. I checked inside and found half a case of fifty-year-old rare Irish whiskey. Using some napkins I found there, I wrapped two bottles so they wouldn't clink against each other and put them in my pack.

Further inspection of the house revealed art—expensive art—in almost every room.

On the south side of the house, a room with a wall of windows was set up as an artist's studio. Van Gogh's *A Wheatfield with Cypresses* sat on an easel. Another easel in front of it held a half-completed copy. An artist's palette and brushes lay on the nearby table. I checked the unfinished forgery and saw the same telltale brushstroke angles Martel had shown me.

Sneaking upstairs, I heard the unmistakable sounds of two people having sex behind one closed door. I listened for a while, and then a woman said something and laughed. Satisfied, I moved down the hall toward the only room with light showing around the door.

The door was ajar a couple of inches, so I took the chance of pushing it farther open so I could see into the room. Gavin O'Bannon lay on a bed. An IV bag hung from a pole next to the bed, along with a couple of electronic monitors. O'Bannon's left shoulder was heavily bandaged, and his chest was wrapped.

A woman stepped into my line of sight. She checked on the IV, checked the monitors, then drifted back out of the picture. A nurse, I assumed. I briefly considered finishing the job, but decided it would be tricky enough escaping the compound without dodging Reagan's thugs.

Slipping out of the house the same way as I had entered, I made my way back to the dock. I briefly considered going back to Victoria in the equipment locker, but that didn't sound like much fun. It would also be pushing my luck.

To add to my problems, a squall had blown in while I was in the house. The wind rustling through the trees provided a prelude to the rain. A flash of lightning out over the water gave me an idea.

In my survey of the property, I had found a large propane tank next to a shed halfway between the back of the house and the wall. Making my way around the house to the shed, I disabled the electronic keypad and opened the door. The generator that supplied electricity for the house was inside.

Pulling out my phone, I called Karen. "Pick me up in half an hour at the place where you dropped me off the other day."

"It's starting to rain, and the waves are picking up."

"Yeah, I know. I'm hoping the storm will mask my escape."

The next time lightning flashed, I placed my hand on the control box, sent an electromagnetic surge into it, and shorted it out. All of the lights all over the compound went out. Backing out of the shed, I headed for the wall.

As I snuck between two of the out buildings, a man opened the door and stepped out into the rain. He turned and shouted back into the house. I couldn't hear it all, but I did catch the phrase, "...that bloody generator..."

I froze in place, hoping he would walk by without noticing me. Instead, he walked directly toward me. To top it off, a flash of lightning highlighted my shape.

When I blurred my form, I blended into the background around me, but I wasn't truly invisible. Light didn't pass through me. As a result, I always avoided having light behind me. The lightning didn't cooperate.

"Who's there?" he called.

I morphed into the form of one of the men I'd seen on the boat in Victoria.

"It's me," I called. "Damned generator's out."

Sometimes your luck is good, and sometimes it's not. He turned on a flashlight and shined it in my face. The man whose form I had copied stepped forward.

"What the hell?" He stared at me with his mouth hanging open.

I kicked him in the stomach. He bent over, and I clubbed him in the back of the head with a two-handed fist. Either I wasn't strong enough, or his head was too hard, but the blow didn't knock him out. He dropped to one knee, and his hand holding the flashlight struck out and caught me in the side. The blow spun me around, and I stumbled and fell.

My father's voice screamed in my mind, *Get up! Get up! Get up!* He had drilled into me over and over that the last place you wanted to be in a fight was on the ground. I rolled away and regained my feet. The sky opened up, and rain fell in a deluge.

My adversary struggled to his feet, but before he could gain his balance, I rushed him again, dropping at the last moment to sweep my leg into his knees. He flew into the air and landed hard on his back and his head. I kicked him in the head, and when his eyes stayed open, I kicked him again.

He lay there, still breathing but not moving. I took off running before anyone else came along. As I ran, I dropped his form and blurred again, trusting to the darkness to hide me.

I had to slow down when I reached the trees. I found a footpath and followed it even as I heard shouting from far behind me. I kept moving, but kept an eye out for any kind of obstacle, such as the tripwire I had found outside the wall. It probably wouldn't have power with the generator down, but if I tripped and broke my skull, it wouldn't matter.

And then the wall loomed in front of me, as smooth and high on the inside as it had appeared from the outside. Shrugging out of my backpack, I fished around inside for my rope and grappling hook.

Luckily, they had trimmed the trees back when they built the wall, but even so, I barely had enough room to swing the hook. It sailed up and over the wall, and I pulled it back slowly. When the rope offered its first resistance, I carefully pulled the hook against the wall and put my weight on it. The hook held.

I climbed up the wall until I reached the top. Turning the hook around, I dropped the rope down the other side and rappelled down, then shook the hook free and retrieved it. I stuffed the rope back in my pack, keeping an eye out for the tripwire. Even so, I almost tripped on it.

Reaching the chain-link fence, I pulled a set of heavy-duty bolt cutters out of my pack and set to work. It would have been easier to climb the fence, but I had no desire to deal with the razor wire. As I worked, I heard voices behind me on the other side of the wall. They sounded confused.

As soon as I cut a hole large enough for me to slip through, I crawled to the other side, then bent the cut section of fence back together. I used a couple of slip-ties to hold it, hoping it would pass a casual inspection. I really didn't want Reagan thinking he'd had an intruder, but that hope was probably dead.

Even though I was fifteen minutes late, Karen was waiting for me, wearing night-vision goggles and cradling a semi-automatic rifle in her arms. I pushed the boat off from the shore and hopped in. I sat there shaking with cold, and she draped a dry blanket over me. We let the boat drift for half an hour, and didn't start the engine until we were well away from Reagan's compound.

When we got back to Victoria, we took showers and changed into dry clothes. I was too exhausted to go out, so we ordered from room service. With the help of Reagan's thousand-credit-a-bottle whiskey, it tasted great.

CHAPTER 16

"All of your paintings are there," I said. I had called Martel, Chung, and Wil together for a meeting. Boyle's office at the Gallery had an alcove with comfortable chairs and two couches overlooking the bay. Fenton was purposely left off the guest list. Cops tend to be so literal about the law.

"What do you mean, 'all of our paintings'?" Chung asked.

"*A Wheatfield with Cypresses, Susanna and the Elders, Storm on the Sea of Galilee*, and the originals of all the forgeries Mr. Martel has identified here at the Gallery."

Chung and Martel simply blinked at me. Wil sat back in his chair, brow wrinkled, and took a sip of his coffee.

"Wait," Martel said, "I thought *Storm on the Sea of Galilee* was at another place here in Vancouver. Has it been stolen again?"

"I'm pretty sure the original is at Reagan's, and the one the Robertsons bought from him is a fake."

"Oh, dear God," Myron breathed. "Fake Rembrandts, too?"

"Just a guess on my part," I said. "But I saw the same painting hanging in two different houses in the past month. Fake Van Goghs, too. The forger is in the process of copying *A Wheatfield with Cypresses*."

Chung and Martel both groaned.

"You know the odd angle of the brushstrokes you showed me?" I asked Martel. He nodded. "I figured that out. The forger is left handed."

Wil gave me a wry smile and said, "I assume this

forger has a name."

I nodded. "Kieran Murphy."

His eyebrows shot up.

"I also found Langston Boyle's killer," I said. "Gavin O'Bannon is at Reagan's, recovering from a gunshot wound." I looked straight at Wil. "Is that enough to get you and Fenton off your asses to search the place?"

"How do we prove he's the killer?"

"Because I saw him do it. If you can recover the bullet I put in O'Bannon, that's added credence to my story."

Chung said, "Director Wilberforce, if you need any backing to hit Reagan's place, we're talking well over a billion credits in insured stolen merchandise. I guarantee he doesn't have that much clout."

⊕⊕⊕

My meeting with Wil and Inspector Fenton didn't go quite as well, but in the end Fenton agreed to working with the Chamber. Forty-eight hours later, I boarded a helicopter in the rain, along with Wil, Fenton, Karen, and eight Chamber SWAT soldiers.

Six helicopters and a coastal guard ship that usually patrolled against piracy comprised quite an operation. But as we flew across the Georgia Strait, we received a radio message from observers stationed on the island across from Reagan's place that his yacht had set sail. Ten minutes later, word came that his jetcopter had taken off.

"Of course, that's probably just coincidence," I shouted to Wil over the roar of the helicopter engine. "There couldn't have been a leak anywhere."

I shut up after that because of the look he gave

me, and the distance to the water below. I knew he wouldn't throw me out, but he was angry enough I didn't want to chance it. The rain pounded on us, and I didn't envy the pilot, who constantly fought the controls as the copter bounced around like a pinball.

I had briefed the commanders and pilots on my observations of the security setup. Karen added her thoughts. The overriding weakness, everyone agreed, was the generator.

A jetcopter carrying an assault team of twelve men dropped into the compound and landed on the abandoned helipad. Men streamed out of the copter just as men streamed out of the mansion and surrounding houses. The Chamber men were better armed, better armored, and better trained. A short, sharp firefight ended with Wil's men capturing the generator and shutting it down.

"Going in," our pilot told us over the intercom. We skimmed over the beach and the front lawn, stopping and hovering directly in front of the house. I checked my pistol as the SWAT guys jumped out of the aircraft, then followed them.

In the face of overwhelming force, Reagan's security guards quickly surrendered. I found the security center in the basement of the mansion and shut it all down.

"Wil, tell your guys to turn the generator back on," I said as I unplugged the last of the equipment.

Once that was done, I cautiously climbed the stairs to the upper level and then to the bedroom wing. With three SWAT team members, we leapfrogged down the hallway checking the bedrooms. It was rather anticlimactic when I found O'Bannon's room empty.

The IV poles and monitors still stood by the bed,

but no IV bag hung there. Doing a quick check of the room, I didn't find any IV bags, or drugs, syringes, bandaging materials, or anything else I expected.

Interrogation of the staff confirmed that Reagan, Kieran, and O'Bannon, along with a doctor and O'Bannon's nurse, had been on the jetcopter. To make matters worse, the storm interfered with radar, and we had no idea where they had gone.

The pirate-hunter ship headed south after Reagan's yacht, which had its own helipad. A seaplane dispatched to find the yacht reported such terrible weather and fog that it turned back to Victoria.

"We lost them, didn't we?" I asked Wil.

"Looks like it."

I led him into the study and showed him the Rembrandts. "At least they didn't make off with these," I said.

The dining room was another matter. Half a dozen of the stolen impressionist paintings I had seen a few nights before were gone. The Van Gogh in Kieran's studio was also gone, as was the unfinished copy. Some of the staff Reagan left behind said that his security guards carried paintings to the boat until about an hour before we arrived, then left in a hurry.

After a prolonged search, I found the safe in Reagan's study. He didn't believe in electronic locks, so it took me about twenty minutes to crack it. Other than for curiosity's sake, I shouldn't have bothered. It was as empty as a banker's conscience.

⊕⊕⊕

Martel and Chung flew out to Reagan's estate the following morning. Along with their staffs, they cataloged all of the artwork they found. The final inventory included more than two dozen stolen paintings, including the Rembrandts, plus statuary, tapestries, and rare books. Reagan had legitimately purchased some of the art in the house, but he would have a hard time proving ownership of the majority of it.

I was in the study checking out the books when Myron found me.

"Libby, nice work. Thank you."

With a shrug, I said, "We only recovered one of your paintings."

"The most valuable one. You also recovered another Rembrandt. It's a lot more than anyone expected."

I had to smile at that. "Didn't you have faith in me, Myron?"

He poured himself some of Reagan's liquor, sat in an overstuffed chair and said, "I did. My superiors were, shall we say, highly skeptical."

"You stuck your neck out?"

"A little, perhaps."

I decided to join him and poured myself a glass.

"Wil says that Reagan's probably headed back to Ireland," I said. "I assume he'll rendezvous with his yacht at some point. Beyond that, who knows?"

"It will take him a long time to sail that far," Myron said.

"He'll probably hop a plane somewhere. Hell, maybe he'll just sit in Japan for a year, then come back here as though nothing has happened."

Myron snorted, then started coughing. When he finished, he said, "Wait until I finish swallowing before you say things like that."

⊕⊕⊕

I spent that night at Wil's hotel. The next morning as we enjoyed a leisurely room-service breakfast, he asked, "So, when do you plan to be back in Toronto?"

"A couple of weeks," I said. I still had to crate up the paintings I'd taken from Abramowitz's flat so I could ship them. I planned on letting Dad market them for me.

"Oh? What have you got going here?"

"I need to pack everything up and make arrangements to ship it. I would also love to see Sheila Robertson's face when she finds out her Rembrandt is a fake. And then the train trip is seven days."

"Aw, come on, Libby. You'd really rather spend seven days on a train when you can fly home in an afternoon?"

"Yep. Safer that way. Prettier, too." A storm had downed an airplane near Atlanta the previous week. Not to mention that airports got far too excited about weapons, explosives, and certain electronic gear. "Come with me. We can spend the whole time in bed."

"Tempting as that is, I need to get back to work," he said.

"Your loss. Well, maybe we'll both be in Toronto at the same time."

"What do you mean?" he asked in a very cautious way.

"I don't plan to stay in Toronto for too long. I'm going to Ireland."

"And why are you going there?"

"Because I have unfinished business with Michael Reagan, Kieran Murphy, and especially Gavin O'Bannon."

"Do you plan to take the train?"

⊕⊕⊕

CHAPTER 17

During the train ride back to Toronto, I asked my father to do some in-depth research on Michael Reagan.

Upon my arrival, Dad picked me and the paintings up, and we drove to his house. I carried the artwork into the house and showed it to him, then carried it all down to the vault in the subbasement.

While he cooked dinner, he told me about Reagan.

"You know he's the head of the organized crime family in Ireland, right? His father and grandfather were in the business. His father also was an amateur painter with some talent, and Michael gained an appreciation for art."

He turned on a blender and made a lot of noise for a little while, poking at whatever he was blending with a long wooden spoon and then blending it again. He nodded and pored the contents into a bowl.

"Michael was considerably more ambitious than his father, and when he inherited the business, he consolidated the other Irish gangs. Word on the street is that after observing his methods of consolidating his main rival, the rest of the gangs were only too glad to join him."

A cutting board, knife, and bowl of vegetables appeared on the table in front of me. "I know you can't cook worth a damn, but you do know how to use a knife. Slice those up."

I dutifully began slicing vegetables while he went back to whatever he was stirring on the stove and continued his story.

"His ambition extended to art collecting. A couple

of my informants tell me that he has a real passion for art. Unfortunately, his tastes and his bank account were at odds. So, he began commissioning works that he wanted. That also led him to brokering some pieces."

Commissioning was parlance for paying someone like me a million credits to steal a fifty million-credit artwork.

"And then he found a talented forger," I said.

"So it seems. It's brilliant, actually," Dad said. "Commission a high-value piece, make a copy of it, sell the copy, and you make money while adding to your collection."

He took the chopped vegetables and put them in a pot on the stove. The kitchen was starting to smell really good and my mouth began to water.

"Anyway," Dad said, "He was making billions, spread into Scotland, and then ran into some resistance. A couple of years ago, he barely escaped an assassination attempt and decided to hide out in Vancouver for a while."

"What are his main businesses?"

"The usual. Drugs, human trafficking, arms. His cover business to give him legitimacy is the same as yours—security. He provides men as security guards, short and long term, in addition to installing and monitoring security systems. If gives him an excuse to keep a private army."

"And now he's back in Ireland."

"Not yet, or at least, not that anyone knows. But his rivals in Scotland and Northern England suffered unexpected accidents recently, shortly before your friend O'Bannon turned up in Vancouver."

"So, if he does go back to Ireland, where would he

go?" I asked.

Dad chuckled, and a screen on the kitchen wall came to life. Some of the billionaire corporate executives built incredibly luxurious houses, but what I saw on the screen surpassed anything I had seen in Canada.

"Castletown House," Dad said. "One of the largest palaces ever built in Ireland. Completed around 1729 and remodeled about thirty years later. It was owned by the government in the twentieth century, but when the Irish government collapsed in 2087, a corporate executive bought it. It's changed hands a couple of times, and Reagan bought it about fifteen years ago. The interesting thing about the house is the legend that it's haunted."

"Ghosts?" I wondered what kind of mutant might imitate a ghost.

"No, the devil himself. The legend goes back hundreds of years."

"Where is it?"

"A little less than an hour west of Dublin. Maybe thirty or forty minutes from the airport on the main cross-country highway. He also has a place in Dublin, but it's not as showy."

"Wife? Kids?"

"Acknowledged children by three different women. Two sons and a daughter. The oldest son is a vice president of his security business. The daughter spends her time partying in Europe. The younger son is a teenager at a boarding school. I found evidence of a wife, but that was thirty years ago and no mention of her since. Reagan doesn't mix with the corporate crowd, but he does socialize with the arts set." He handed me a chip. "Everything I turned up is here."

Wil flew in two days later and took me to dinner.

"I've put out a world-wide watch for Reagan, Murphy and O'Bannon," he said as we waited to be seated at my favorite restaurant. "The yacht docked in Vietnam, and Murphy was spotted on deck. No telling where they'll go next."

The hostess escorted us to our table. Wil ordered wine, then said, "No comment?"

"I'm thinking. Can't you hear the gears grinding together?"

He smiled and waited. After our meals came, I said, "It wouldn't hurt to go to Ireland before they get there. I can scout things out and make some contacts. But it doesn't make sense to go there if they don't. Maybe when we have a better idea about where they're going and when they're going to get there."

I called Dad the next day. "It looks like my trip to Ireland will be delayed. Reagan is taking the long way around to get home."

⊕⊕⊕

With time on my hands, I checked with Dad and found seven backed-up orders for security system installations. Figuring that Vietnam was a long way from Ireland, I took the largest job first. At that point, I remembered why I had been so willing to jump at Myron's offer, other than the money, of course. Work was a lot of work. And while I was good at all the ordering of equipment, tracking invoices, and keeping the books straight, I didn't enjoy it. For the first time, I thought about hiring someone.

I did enjoy the design work, and there was something soothing about the physical part of the work. It didn't take long to fall back into the pattern of my pre-Vancouver life.

The thing I did enjoy the most was seeing my friend Nellie and hearing her sing. The night I got into town, after I had dinner with Dad, I went down to The Pinnacle. When I walked in, Nellie was on stage belting out an Ella Fitzgerald song. I strolled over to the bar, and Paul Renard, my other best friend, gave out a whoop. He rushed around the bar and scooped me up in a hug.

"Damn, Libby. I never thought I'd say it, but I missed you."

I kissed him on the forehead. "No one to give you a hard time?"

"Oh, just the usual, but things have been kind of boring around here. No one getting blown up, no mass murders," he dropped his voice and whispered in my ear, "no uber-rich corporate types wailing about their toys disappearing."

He pulled back and smiled. "What are you drinking?"

I heard Nellie's voice falter. Both Paul and I looked toward the stage, and saw her staring back at us with a huge smile on her face. She picked up the lyrics again, but her gaze was locked on me, as mine was locked on her.

She finished the song and jumped off the stage just as I was taking the first sip of my drink. Dark hair flying behind her, she skipped across the room on stiletto heels like a ballerina. Paul's hug had been very tight, but I thought little Nellie would crush my ribs. Absolutely uninhibited, she buried her face between my breasts and inhaled deeply.

"Oh, God, I have missed you," she said. She pulled my head down and kissed me with a lot of tongue.

When she finally let me up for air, I managed to gasp, "I missed you, too."

I didn't get much sleep that night, so I was fairly fuzzy when we arrived at my mom's restaurant for brunch the next day. Mom knew I was coming into town, so I probably shouldn't have been surprised when Glenda, the street urchin I had semi-adopted, came flying out of the kitchen.

"Miz Libby!" she squealed, giving my poor ribs one more crushing squeeze. There was a lot more of her than when she first came to live with Mom. It was more like hugging a girl than a little kid.

"Are you working?" I asked. Mom and Dominick, her partner, had given Glenda a job in the kitchen.

"No, not until later," she said.

"Have you had breakfast yet?"

She said she had eaten earlier, but didn't argue when I urged her to sit down with Nellie and me. Glenda spent most of her first fifteen years on the verge of starvation, and it seemed like you could never fill her up.

We ordered, and then I asked, "So, how are your studies going?" Teaching her to read and write and do arithmetic was a project shared by Nellie and me along with just about everyone who worked for Mom.

"I'm reading a book," Glenda announced. The pride on her face brought tears to my eyes.

"What's it about?" Nellie asked.

"It's not about anything. It's a made-up story."

"Oh? What's the story about?" I asked.

"A kid named Harry Potter. He's a wizard." Her face screwed up in concentration. "I think a wizard is a kind of mutant. But it's just make believe. You know? I seen a lotta mutants, and I never seen anyone

152

wave a magic wand to make things happen. I have to look a lot of the words up in the dictionary, but it's a lotta fun. Betsy gave it to me."

Betsy was Nellie's younger sister.

While we were eating, Mom came in and sat with us. It felt good to be with family. I hadn't realized that I'd missed them so much.

⊕⊕⊕

Wil's contacts helped us track Reagan's progress around the world. A Chamber operative managed to sneak onto the yacht in the Mediterranean, and reported that Reagan and Murphy were on board, but O'Bannon was not. I booked my ticket to Ireland the next day.

"You don't even know he's in Ireland," Wil protested as he watched me pack.

"No, but I'll bet Reagan shipped him out to a hospital, if not in Ireland, then in Switzerland or someplace else in Europe."

"If Reagan didn't decide he was a liability and dump him in the ocean somewhere."

"Possible, but I doubt it. If he wanted to get rid of O'Bannon, the time to do it was when he first got shot. Dump the body in the Strait of Georgia and walk away."

I finished packing the second of the two boxes with equipment I couldn't take on an airplane. My dad had set up shipping for them through an old friend of his at MegaTech, the company he worked for before he retired. Hauling my suitcases out, I began pulling clothes from my closet.

"You'll call me if you find O'Bannon, right?" Wil asked.

Surprised, I turned to him. "Why?"

"I can't worry about you all the time," he said, "it's just too exhausting. But if you find O'Bannon, or Reagan gets to Ireland, I'll know it's time to start."

Walking over to him, I took his face in my hands and kissed him. "If it makes you happy, then I'll call you."

"Promise? Or are you lying to me?"

"Promise."

CHAPTER 18

Stepping off the plane at Dublin Airport, I sniffed the air, expecting to smell the ocean. In spite of being only a few miles from the Irish Sea, my nose detected only verdant vegetation and jet fuel.

Once the taxi took me beyond the airport, I could see why. Everything was so green. Not just the green of Toronto or Vancouver, but every shade of green I could imagine. Bushes and trees were trimmed away from the roadway, but hung over the top of us. It looked as if we drove through a green tunnel.

Dublin had never built skyscrapers, so the churches had been the tallest buildings. It made me sad to see the spires of the old cathedrals poking up through the waters of the bay. Half-submerged buildings—houses, hotels, office buildings, and shops—lined both shores of the River Liffey and the bay.

Much of old Dublin was gone. The city had escaped the nuclear destruction of so many of the world's major metropolises, but the oceans' rise drowned most of the major Irish cities. Scientists projected that in another two or three hundred years, if the rest of the Antarctic and Greenland ice melted, Ireland would be more of an archipelago than an island.

I met the landlady at the home I rented online and got the key code. The end-of-group townhouse dated to the mid-twenty-first century, and though it needed some maintenance and updating, it otherwise met the advertisement, and it was clean. It was near bus and train lines, as well as downtown and the university. I paid three months' rent in advance.

After talking with Wil, I decided to skip renting a

car. The Irish still maintained the antiquated habit of driving on the wrong side of the road. I figured it would be simpler and less stressful to rent a motorcycle. A bus line passed a block from the flat, so I took the bus to the motorcycle store.

The balding guy with a beer belly I had to deal with didn't seem to think women knew how to ride one of his precious machines.

"Hi. I'm Jasmine Keller. I arranged to lease an ElectroRocket."

He eyed me, spending a little too long on my chest. "Well, now, that's a very powerful motorcycle," he said. "I think you'd probably find it easier to handle one of those TownScooters."

"Thank you for your concern, but I own an older model of the ElectroRocket, and that's what I want."

He asked for a deposit equal to the sales price of the bike and smirked at me.

I wanted to wipe the smirk off his face, but he had Jasmine's identification, and I really wanted to keep that identity unspoiled. A bus ride to the suburbs south of the city took an hour and a half, but the shop there rented me a bike without giving me a hassle.

Driving on the left wasn't a problem on the motorway, but I figured out quickly that the Irish seemed to have missed the invention of the stop sign. They were absolutely in love with roundabouts.

By the time I got back to the house, I needed a drink. Unfortunately, I hadn't had time to visit any food or liquor stores. Luckily, there was some kind of law about always having a pub within walking distance.

The next morning, I called my dad's contact and arranged to have my equipment delivered. That happened around noon, and I spent the afternoon setting up the security system, file server, and network. With that taken care of, I started looking for O'Bannon.

It had been almost two months since I shot the assassin. I didn't know the extent of his injuries, but I figured that he was probably close to being healed. A search online showed that he owned a townhouse in Dublin and a country house near Cork. The other obvious places to look for him would be at Reagan's Castletown House estate near Celbridge, or Reagan's mansion in North Dublin. The Dublin house was Reagan's main home. From what I could determine, Castletown was used primarily for entertaining.

O'Bannon's neighborhood in Dublin was several steps up from the neighborhood where I rented. Lots of hip pubs and restaurants, boutique shops, and a young, well-to-do crowd. It was easy to find his house, and I scouted it as much as I could during the day.

My dad's research said that O'Bannon liked fine foods—especially Italian and French—expensive wines, and women of a particular physical type. Adopting a form of a woman that matched his taste, I checked out a couple of wine bars, and then had dinner at a very expensive French restaurant only a block away from his house.

Cruising the pubs in the neighborhood that night didn't turn him up, so when the hour grew late and the crowds thinned, I slipped into an alley, blurred my form, and snuck up on his house.

There didn't appear to be anyone home, so I bypassed the security system and entered through the back door. It didn't take long to learn that he wasn't in residence, and hadn't been for a while. Nothing in the refrigerator, no dirty laundry. The only thing of

157

interest was the gun safe in the basement.

The electronic lock took only a moment. The safe held two rifles and three pistols. One of the rifles was of a type used for competitive target shooting. The other was a fifty-caliber sniper rifle with a high-powered telescope. The kind of gun used for extremely long-range shots. I left everything where it was and closed the safe.

As I let myself out, I reflected that if I were recuperating, I'd probably choose a house in the country rather than a noisy part of the city.

The following day, I drove out to Celbridge, the town nearest to Reagan's Castletown House. I acted like a completely clueless tourist, pretending I thought the manor was still accessible to the public. I soon learned that Reagan wasn't on the best of terms with his neighbors. Basically, no one had anything good to say about anyone associated with Castletown.

I rode out to the residential area that abutted the estate and found a place to park the bike. Slipping into the woods, I quickly reached the fence around the property. It was the kind of fence I hated—fifteen-foot wrought-iron bars topped with spikes. Brick pillars every twelve feet anchored the wrought iron, but the pillars were twelve feet tall with razor wire stretched between the wrought iron on either side. It was clear that Reagan wanted his visitors to use the gates.

CCTV and motion sensors were installed at intervals on the house, but I didn't see any motion sensors around the horse stables or the servants' quarters and the kitchen.

It took a couple of hours to walk around the perimeter, but it turned out that Reagan used the same fencing even far away from the house. I couldn't see any good ways to approach the place.

I spent the next week staking out the house, watching through binoculars, hoping to catch a glimpse of O'Bannon. Neither he nor the nurse from the Vancouver compound made any appearances, though I saw a lot of other people. The landscape crew was extensive, as were men who I assumed were part of the security force. Plus, I counted at least twenty people who appeared to be household staff.

⊕⊕⊕

After two days of rain and wind, I took advantage of the first nice day. The bike ride took five hours to reach O'Bannon's country cottage west of Cork. The countryside was as beautiful and tranquil as all the pictures. Since The Fall and the global increase in temperatures, Ireland had warmed up, but the climate continued to be wetter and cooler than in Canada.

I would never have found O'Bannon's place without a GPS. It was two miles from the nearest village and a quarter-mile from a road barely wide enough for one car. I parked the bike in a copse of trees and followed a low stone wall to get within sight of his house.

It didn't look any different than the other farmhouses in the area. Two stories, and about the same size as his Dublin townhouse. A two-car garage and a ramshackle barn were the only other structures. Other than motion-triggered lights in the front and back, I couldn't spot any evidence of a security system.

On the other hand, a huge pasture of open lawn surrounding the house provided no cover to approach the place. From what I'd seen on my drive down from Dublin, a lot of Ireland's land consisted of low, rolling hills, but O'Bannon's house sat in a very flat part of the country. I ruled out finding a place to hide and stake out the house, or even to use as a sniper's perch.

The place looked deserted. After spending an hour watching for some activity, I rode back to the village I'd passed through and hit the pub across the street from the church. The proprietor served me a bowl of lamb stew and a glass of stout that renewed my faith in the world.

"American?" he asked when he brought my second beer.

"Sort of. Canadian, North American."

"On holiday?"

"Yes. Holiday and business. My firm posted me to Dublin for a project. But on my own time, I want to see the country. A man I met one time told me about this part of Ireland, so here I am."

"And what do you think?"

"It's absolutely beautiful. The only problem is, if people keep feeding me like this, I'll have to buy a new wardrobe."

He beamed. "Was it a local man?"

"I think so. He said he lived northwest of Blarney. I can't remember exactly where. I do remember that he mentioned Ballyandreen, which confused the hell out of me because there are two towns with that name near Cork."

He roared with laughter. "What was this bloke's name?"

"Gavin. I never did get his last name. Tall, burley man, head shaved bald, with a fat nose. Probably in his forties."

The innkeeper tilted his head to the side, obviously thinking. "That would seem to fit a man I know. Gavin O'Bannon. His place is north of here. It's a small world, isn't it?"

"Really? You know him? Does he come in here

160

often?"

"He was away for a while. He travels on business. He's back now, though he seems to stick close to home. Had an accident sometime back. Told me he had a rough time of it."

"That's too bad. Do you think he'll recover?"

"Can't use his left arm very well. Said he crushed the shoulder, broke some ribs, and punctured his lung. Said he's coming back from it, but it's a slow process. If I see him, who should I say?"

I thought furiously. My first temptation was to say Danielle Kincaid, but I bit my tongue. "Jasmine," I said. "Tell him Jasmine from Vancouver asked about him. I doubt he remembers me. We just met in a bar one night."

I used Jasmine's credit card to pay for my meal. "Are there any places that rent rooms near here?"

"Back toward Blarney would be the closest," he said.

I thanked him and left. When I got outside and walked around the side to get my bike, I pumped my fist in the air and screamed, "Yes!"

⊕⊕⊕

I checked into a hotel near Blarney using my real name and form, then went shopping in the village near Blarney castle. I bought a couple of warm sweaters and a long black woolen cloak. The Irish weather was starting to get to me. The natives were walking around in shorts and t-shirts, but the temperatures were barely in the eighties on a nice day.

I found a lovely restaurant touting locally-sourced food, guaranteed non-toxic. I found that easy to believe, as southern Ireland had never been a major polluter. The local salmon I ordered was probably the best I'd ever tasted.

Halfway through my meal, I saw O'Bannon come in. I turned my head away, keeping track of him out of the corner of my eye. As he walked to his table, he glanced my way, and I thought I saw him hesitate. Maybe it was just my imagination, as he recovered quickly. He did, however, take a seat where he could watch me.

I got up and went to the ladies' room. I thought about what O'Bannon might know about me. He had tried to kill Danielle Kincaid. I had shot him, but he never saw me. On the other hand, Kieran Murphy knew me as Libby Nelson in my natural form, and knew I was an insurance investigator. The bartender in Vicarstown also knew me in my natural form, but as Jasmine Keller. I rented the townhouse in Dublin as Jasmine and in the form that matched her identification pictures.

All this made me a little dizzy and I had to sit down. I usually wasn't that careless. Before I went back to my table, I darkened my hair slightly, lengthened it a few inches, and altered its part and style. I also shortened my stature about four inches, modified my facial features, and turned my eyes green. The woman in the mirror resembled Libby Nelson, but wasn't her. It was the best I could do to try to salvage the situation.

O'Bannon watched me as I walked back to my table, but I thought I could see puzzlement, or perhaps uncertainty, in his face. I ignored him, never looking directly at him. I did note that all he ordered was an appetizer and a single glass of wine, then I saw him paying and leaving as I prepared to go.

That made me nervous. I went to the ladies' room again and completely altered my appearance. The

162

woman who walked out of the restaurant was a foot shorter than I was, with a dark complexion, dark hair, and wearing a different color dress. I walked down the street to a hotel and checked in as Suri Selvaskanen.

So, there I was, without a change of clothes or even a toothbrush. My rented motorcycle was parked at the restaurant. And as far as I knew, a homicidal maniac was hanging around the village hoping to end my life.

I waited a few minutes, then blurred my form and took the back stairs out of the hotel. I really wasn't dressed for wandering around in the dark trying to stalk an assassin. I could imagine myself dressed in a black cat suit, but that didn't change the reality that I had put on a dress and two-inch heels to go out to dinner.

Circling around to the restaurant, I scouted the area, hoping to spot O'Bannon. I didn't see him in any of the hiding places that would allow him to watch the restaurant's front door. He might have climbed to a roof, but the bartender's description of O'Bannon's arm caused me to dismiss the idea. Besides, I wasn't dressed for wall climbing.

An hour of searching didn't turn up anything, so I went to get my bike. I froze as I saw it. Both tires had been slashed with a large knife. O'Bannon knew that the woman in the pub and the woman in the restaurant were the same. If he had known I was Danielle Kincaid, I would probably have been dead.

CHAPTER 19

I spent a very nervous morning arranging for a man with a lorry to transport the motorcycle to Cork City. A shop there was the closest place that had tires for the bike. I gathered my things and checked out of the hotel.

It took me an hour to scout the area in my blurred form before I dared to get near the bike. I'm sure the guy who drove me to Cork thought I was weird, as I spent most of the trip hunched down in my seat, keeping my head low. O'Bannon knew the area, and I was sure he could figure out a good ambush spot.

As it turned out, my first attempt to sneak up on O'Bannon was a spectacular failure. I thought through everything I had done since landing in Ireland, and traced every one of my actions and mistakes.

The shop in Cork had the tires and fixed the bike in an hour.

"Those tires look like they were cut," the repairman said.

I gave him a sour look. "Arsehole ex-boyfriend."

He chuckled, but sobered quickly when I snarled at him.

"Need to improve your taste in men."

"No kidding. But after I kill him, there will be one less jerk that I have to worry about."

That sobered him up and ended the questions.

But having found O'Bannon, I wasn't willing to give up. Although the Suri persona was as different from Libby as any two women could be, I hadn't chosen her at random. She exactly matched the physical type of women that my father told me

O'Bannon favored.

Leaving the bike at the repair shop, I rented a car and drove back to Blarney. At Suri's hotel, I extended her stay. In her persona, I toured Blarney Castle and played tourist, settling into being someone so much different and shorter than I was.

That evening, rather than make reservations, I walked into the same restaurant where I'd seen O'Bannon before and waited in the bar for half an hour. I didn't know if O'Bannon would go back to the restaurant, but hoped that his arrogance and curiosity would bring him back.

My hope was rewarded when O'Bannon came in and was shown to a table. Shortly thereafter, the hostess came for me. She led me past O'Bannon to a table behind him. I looked around and asked, "Is it possible to sit over there?"

The table I pointed to was near the kitchen and not as desirable, but it was directly in O'Bannon's line of sight. The hostess shrugged and led me to the other table.

I ordered light and ate delicately, completely the opposite of my normal ravenous approach to food. I did order dessert, though. Throughout my meal, I noticed him staring at me, and when I caught him at it, I blushed, smiled, looked down at my plate, then looked back at him through my eyelashes.

After I finished eating, I ordered tea and asked the waiter, "Is there an establishment near here with musicians who perform Irish music?"

He told me of a nearby pub, and when I acted dumb about his directions, we did a great pantomime with me pointing and gesticulating, then him pointing, and our voices rising enough that people around us could hear.

"And a woman alone," I asked, "it is allowed?"

"Oh, certainly."

"And safe?"

"I assure you," the waiter said, "you will be perfectly safe."

As the waiter walked away, I glanced at O'Bannon, holding his eyes for a few moments. Then I blushed again.

I made my way down the street to the pub, half expecting to hear footsteps behind me. When I reached the door, I glanced back but only saw two couples, laughing together as they walked along.

Once inside, I ordered a cider from the bartender and found a small table that three people were vacating. Taking a seat, I settled in to listen to the music. It was low season, and at least half of the people present looked like locals. The tourists appeared to be mostly older, probably retirees.

About five minutes later, O'Bannon walked in. He made his way across the room, and several people hailed him. The lady bartender greeted him warmly, and they leaned across the bar and bussed each other on the cheek. It was a very different view of the man than my mental image of an assassin and torturer. It suddenly struck me that he was probably a local. Hell, it made sense. Everyone is born somewhere. In my research, I found that O'Bannon owned the house I had seen, but I hadn't found a record of him buying it, as I had with the Dublin townhouse.

He stood at the bar chatting with the bartender for a while, and at one point both looked directly at me. She smiled and laughed and said something to him. Collecting his pint, he walked toward me and stopped at my table.

"Is anyone sitting here?" His voice was a pleasant baritone. That helped, since his physical appearance had a lack of appeal.

"No, no one," I said, my gaze flicking up to him, and then back down.

He pulled out a chair and sat down, setting his beer on the table.

"Are you enjoying the music?" he asked.

"Yes, very much." A new musician joined the group sitting in a circle at the front of the pub. "Are they not a band?"

O'Bannon smiled, revealing white, slightly crooked teeth. It wasn't completely unpleasant. "Just a bunch of local musicians," he said. "Anyone who wants to can show up with an instrument and play."

"Are they not paid?"

"Oh, no. They play for the pleasure of it, just like we listen. Where are you from?"

I don't know why I wasn't prepared for that question, but it seemed I wasn't ready for O'Bannon on a number of levels. A recent documentary on immigrant communities in Australia popped into my head.

"Australia."

"I haven't been there," he said, and I breathed a sigh of relief. "Are you here on business or holiday?"

We continued with a completely banal conversation the rest of the evening. When the musicians packed up, the customers followed them. O'Bannon offered to walk me back to my hotel.

For a brief moment, I thought I might get him alone and kill him. Unfortunately, the street was crowded, and many of the pub's patrons were staying at the same hotel I was. I flirted with the idea of inviting him up to my room, but he had yet to touch me, and I decided that he might be suspicious of such an offer.

So, I let him walk me home. At the hotel, I turned to him and said, "Thank you for a very pleasant evening, Gavin. I enjoyed it very much."

"I'm glad," he said. "How long will you be in Blarney?"

"Several more days. Do you have any recommendations for tours I might take?"

He bit. "If you would like, I can play your tour guide. I grew up around here, and I can show you anything you're interested in."

I did the coy look-down-then-back-up-through-my-lashes thing, and in a voice so soft he had to lean close to hear me, said, "That is a very gallant offer, but I wouldn't want to inconvenience you. I'm sure you have more important things to do than chauffeur me around."

"As a matter of fact, I'm convalescing from an injury, and I have little to do. It would be good for me to get out and about."

Raising my eyes, I gave him a smile. "I would enjoy your company very much."

"I'll be here at nine in the morning," he said, and walked off with a bounce in his step. He held his left arm very stiffly at his side.

Even though I did not intend to let him get too close, I wondered what kind of kinks he had. Suppressing a shudder, I went up to my room.

⊕⊕⊕

O'Bannon showed up on time the following morning. Suri appeared wearing a red wrap blouse, white pants, a scarf to contain her hair, and a short black cloak with a hood. In reality, I wore a black catsuit, its pockets stuffed with lethal equipment, and the long black cloak I had purchased a couple of days before.

"You look very lovely," he said in greeting. I lowered my eyes and blushed. "Where would you like to go on this pleasant day?"

I shot an involuntary look at the gray sky above and decided that he was crazy. Or maybe the Irish were. It wasn't raining yet, so maybe that's what he meant.

"Among the places I wanted to see is the park at Killarney," I said. "Is that too far?"

"Absolutely not. A splendid suggestion."

He led me to a red sports car and opened the door for me. I had thought long about where to go. Hopefully, Killarney National Park would provide plenty of opportunities for isolation, and a train ran from the town of Killarney to Cork. I could pick up the motorcycle, and be gone before anyone found the body. Nice and clean.

We drove through some more beautiful country, but I was becoming convinced that everywhere in Ireland was beautiful. O'Bannon cheerfully talked about the countryside we drove through, other interesting facts about Ireland, and in general, was a pleasant companion. Inside, I was a bundle of nerves. Sitting beside a man who had come within inches of killing me was incredibly uncomfortable. I hoped he thought my nervousness was simply that of a woman on a first date.

That thought made me even more nervous. I had chosen the Suri persona because it matched what I'd been told about O'Bannon's physical preferences. But

169

what kind of woman would climb in a car with a total stranger in a strange country? O'Bannon seemed to think it was natural. I thought it was weird that he thought so.

We reached the town of Killarney in less than two hours. He asked if I was hungry, and we stopped at a pub for lunch. After a stroll around the town, we drove out to Ross Castle.

"Can we take a walk?" I asked. Indicating the lake, I started to my left, away from the parking lot, visitor center, and castle, which looked like a shoebox set on end.

"Of course." His smile showed a little surprise, but he seemed pleased.

We walked along a path, and when it petered out, I continued into the woods. O'Bannon walked by my side, answering my questions about various trees, the lake and the park.

"It's very beautiful," I said, gazing out over the lake. "Thank you for bringing me here."

I suddenly stopped, and he took a couple of steps before realizing I wasn't beside him anymore. He turned back toward me, and I shot him in the chest. He staggered backwards, splashing into the water, and fell.

Walking to the edge of the water, I watched his body slowly float away in a spreading red cloud. I shuddered, and the tension flowed out of me. The feeling of relief was almost overwhelming.

I put my pistol away, morphed into a sixty-year-old man, and walked swiftly back to the visitor center. An hour later, I boarded a tour bus with a bunch of other old people, and rode into town. A few of the other riders gave me odd looks, I assumed because I hadn't been on the bus earlier, but I ignored them.

Once I reached Killarney, I morphed into Danielle Kincaid and bought a train ticket to Cork. By evening, I had my motorcycle, a room in a hotel, and a seat in a pub listening to live music while eating dinner.

During a break in the music, I pulled out my phone and called Wil.

"Hi. Heard anything new about Reagan and Murphy?"

"Hi, yourself. Enjoying Ireland?"

"I am. Wil, it's beautiful here. I want to come back sometime with you."

"That's an invitation I'll take you up on. Any luck finding Gavin O'Bannon?"

"He had an accident. What about Reagan and Murphy?"

There was silence on the other end of the phone, and then I heard him sigh. "They docked in England yesterday."

"Sounds like they're coming home. Let me know when they set sail again."

⊕⊕⊕

Wil called the next morning. "Are you in Dublin?"

"Yeah, why?"

"I'm at the airport. Come pick me up."

"I hope you're traveling light. I don't have a car, only a motorcycle."

Silence, then, "Okay, I guess I'll rent a car. Where are you?"

I gave him my address. "What are you doing in Dublin?"

"I'll see you when I get there," he responded and hung up, leaving me to speculate on what he was doing.

By the time he arrived at my door two hours later, I had decided he was either coming to play hero, or he thought he needed to rein me in. Or both.

In any case, it really didn't matter why he'd come, I was happy to see him. We played kissy-face when he arrived and spent the afternoon in bed. Dinner at the pub across the street was followed by more bed.

"So," I said the following morning, "you came to Dublin just because you were horny?"

He laughed. "We have word that Reagan will be arriving here sometime later today or this evening."

"You could have sent me an email."

"More fun this way."

I had to laugh at that.

"I've been in touch with the local Chamber," Wil said. "They have the marina where he docks his boat under surveillance, and we'll have a team meet him when he lands. I don't want those paintings to get away."

"Sounds good to me," I said, rolling over and burrowing deeper into the covers.

"You don't object?"

"Why should I? I get paid whether I retrieve the paintings alone or if an army helps me."

CHAPTER 20

Wil and I spent the early part of the day sightseeing after eating a full Irish breakfast. Bacon, sausages, an egg, black and white pudding, a fried tomato, fried mushrooms, and toast with butter. And it was cheap! It amazed me that anyone on the island weighed under four hundred pounds if they ate that every morning.

We sat around with half a dozen Chamber men in a café overlooking the marina where Reagan leased a boat slip, drank coffee, and waited. As afternoon turned to evening, I began to get antsy.

"Is there any way to know where he is?" I asked. It bothered me that Wil managed to put an operative on board Reagan's ship in France, but the guy didn't plant a tracker on the ship. I wondered if I could sell training services to the Chamber.

"We had a satellite image of the boat near Wales," Wil said, "but things clouded up, and we lost him."

I looked up at a typical gray, drizzling Irish sky and sighed. Depending on the weather in Ireland was a little bit like depending on a boyfriend. If you wanted to get pissed on, it was dependable.

By the time it got dark, Wil was starting to show as much impatience as I felt. Around midnight, one of the Chamber men came in and announced that Reagan had docked at Belfast, unloaded, and disappeared.

Wil looked at me as though I were going to explode and take the whole group with me.

"I don't know about the rest of you," I said, "but I've had enough coffee to float an oil tanker. Anyone know a good place to get a drink?"

We trooped down the street and into a pub. As we entered the place, Wil leaned into me and said, "I thought you'd be more upset."

"You don't know me as well as you think you do," I said. "Patience is a virtue. Once I staked out a target for weeks, only to have him fly to South America. Reagan didn't get to where he is by being stupid."

"We'll get him," Wil said.

I gave him my best raised-eyebrow look, which I knew wasn't half as good as his. "We'll talk."

And then I settled down to an appreciation of some good Irish whiskey and a couple of beers that the Irish called 'mother's milk'.

⊕⊕⊕

Over breakfast the next morning, I filled Wil in on the scouting trip I had taken out to Reagan's estate.

"I don't know what kind of defenses he has beyond the alarms and surveillance," I said after detailing the security setup, "but depending on how many men he can deploy, it might be rather dangerous to go in after him. I assume that your Chamber buddies here in Ireland would love to nail him, but I notice they haven't done much."

"People like Reagan are adept at deniability," Wil said. "You don't find them going out and pulling the trigger themselves, or kidnapping teenagers and selling them as prostitutes. That's why I was able to get the resources for this operation. He's actually touching the art. If we can nail him in possession of millions in stolen art, and especially if we can tie him to the forgeries, then we can bring him down."

I thought about it, then said, "What if I could find evidence in his computer systems? You know, emails, bank account transactions, stuff like that? Stuff that

174

ties him to illegal activities or even to murders?"

Wil shook his head. "Breaking into his systems, or his bank's system, is as illegal as his activities." He held up his hand when I opened my mouth. "Libby, no corporation is completely clean, and the rules are set up to protect them unless they really step over the line. We're not allowed to use computer evidence unless we already have enough other evidence to bust them."

"I didn't know you needed evidence to persecute someone you don't like," I grumbled.

He leaned across the table and kissed me on the forehead. "I don't. I can persecute anyone I want, but I have to abide by the rules of evidence if I want to prosecute them. If I had the resources, I could set twenty people to following Reagan around day and night and make his life miserable. But he'd just fly somewhere else, and my budget can't match his. That's where prosecution is superior. I just lock him in a cage."

He gave me a side-eyed look. "You haven't been breaking into his systems or his bank, have you?"

I rolled my eyes. I used to think his naiveté was endearing, but he really should have known better than to ask that question.

"Just a surface scan," I said, and watched his expression change to one of alarm. "His accounts are so tangled that it would take months to figure everything out. Covers and fronts and cut-outs, companies that don't exist paying companies that do exist, and owners that aren't owners. Either he's a genius at generating confusion, or he employs one."

"So why did you even ask about hacking his systems?"

"Because he keeps the art deals separate. The

buyers and sellers are coded, but if we traced the money, I could probably figure it out."

He looked thoughtful. "Well, I can't use such information to prosecute him, but I'm sure the insurance companies would be interested, and they wouldn't care how you got it."

I shook my head. Wil was a bright guy, but he didn't seem to understand how the world worked.

"Wil, if I told Myron Chung that I could access bank information, he'd have a contract on me before morning. You just don't tell big corporations information that makes them feel threatened. An insurance company can employ a cat burglar or an assassin without a twinge of conscience. Elite hackers are on everyone's shoot-on-sight list."

A light went on. I could see it in his eyes.

We drove out to Reagan's that afternoon. Compared to my previous visit, the place was bustling. Wil brought a drone with him, and sent it into the sky, then we sat back, drank coffee, and watched the screen. We saw cars and trucks coming and going along the roads leading to the estate. People inside the fence hustled back and forth. Guards made their rounds. Basically, it looked like the boss was home.

"You haven't been inside?" Wil asked.

"No. I might be able to slip through the gate when it's open, but only at night. Going over the fence is a non-starter."

He chuckled. "Must drive you crazy to find a place you can't break into."

"I didn't say that. It will just take a little longer. We need to check if he's hiring anyone."

Wil turned toward me. "And?"

"And I get hired. Doesn't matter what kind of job

they're looking for. If not, then we find someone critical and convince them to quit. Instant job opening."

With a laugh, he said, "And if they're looking for a cook?"

"Absolutely no problem. There will be a lot of collateral damage, though. To make sure I get him, I'll have to poison everyone, not just him."

He choked on his coffee.

"Actually," I said, "I'm hoping he'll throw a party."

For a moment, I thought Wil might choke again. "What? Why in the world would he do that?"

"Ego. That house is full of art, and he brought a bunch of new stuff home with him. It won't be as much fun if he can't show it off."

"All the new stuff is stolen!"

"So? That didn't bother all those rich people in Vancouver. You should know better. The rules are made by the rich and powerful to control everyone else. It's been that way throughout history, and nothing has changed."

We sat there and watched the screen and brainstormed. Wil suddenly zoomed the camera in on the side door on the right side of the main house. I caught a flash of copper, then the camera steadied. Kieran Murphy, dressed to go horseback riding, walked along the portico to the stables.

"That's an idea," I said.

"What is?"

"When she goes out, we could kidnap her, and I'll take her place."

Wil continued to stare at the screen as though I hadn't spoken. We watched Kieran enter the stables, then he leaned back and turned to me.

"What makes you think she'll go out?"

"A couple of things. She has family north of Dublin that she hasn't seen in a couple of years, and she can't have much of a wardrobe. I mean, how many clothes can you take on a boat when you leave in a raging hurry?"

He seemed to think about it. "You said she and Reagan are intimate."

"She's screwing him. I don't know about how intimate they are."

"Don't you think he'll notice that you aren't her? I mean, they just spent a couple of months on a small ship together. She would know a lot of things that might trip you up."

I shrugged. "Possibly."

Someone on horseback emerged from the rear of the stables. Wil aimed the drone's camera, and we could see Kieran's strawberry blonde hair flowing down her back.

"Even if he doesn't notice, what are you going to do if he gets amorous?" Wil asked.

"I'm sorry honey. I have a headache."

"You don't get headaches. Suppose Kieran doesn't either?"

"That's because I like you." I did not want the conversation to go in that direction. He could be a little prudish sometimes, and I definitely didn't want to deal with any possessiveness. Especially when it came to business. "Hell, Wil, I just need to get inside. If the paintings are there, I call you and you come riding in like the cavalry."

He shook his head. "I think that's a lousy idea. Suppose the paintings aren't there? How do you plan to get out?"

178

"Then we draw Reagan out, and I go in while he's gone."

"And how are we going to do that?"

"Stage an art show. One that will pique their interest, and send them an invitation. We can even organize a charity show, invite all the rich thieves, and donate the money to a good cause."

"And you think that will work?"

"I'm very interested in better ideas." I put my chin on my fist, leaned forward, and gazed wide-eyed at him, waiting for him to enlighten me. I waited a long time, then poured myself some more coffee.

CHAPTER 21

Wil and I were out running one morning when his phone rang. He spoke with someone for a few minutes, and when he hung up, he said, "Your buddy O'Bannon got out of the hospital."

"Huh?"

"You told me he had an accident. Well, I guess he's well enough to travel. He checked out this morning."

"That's impossible." Wil cocked his head and raised an eyebrow. "Wil, I shot him. Right through the chest. He was less than ten feet away. Really. He died. Fell in the lake and floated away. I know what a dead man looks like."

Wil got back on his phone. Fifteen minutes later, he said, "According to local authorities in Killarney, one Gavin O'Bannon was found floating in the lake, Lough Leane. He'd been shot in the chest, and the bullet exited his back. They took him to the local hospital, and although he was close to bleeding out, he survived. The bullet missed his heart, lungs, and spine. In other words, it didn't hit anything vital." He shook his head. "That's incredible. He must be the luckiest man alive."

"So where is he now?"

"Some men picked him up at the hospital and headed north on the road to Limerick."

I normally tried not to curse, too much, but I had paid attention to the creative way my father sometimes used language. I tried some of it out. It really didn't make me feel better, but it did relieve some tension. Wil looked shocked.

Back at the townhouse, I took a shower, then

turned the bathroom over to Wil. With a towel wrapped around my hair, I rummaged in the freezer for a quiche to microwave, and turned on the screen to check the weather.

The major story on every news site was a variation of, "Art Scandal in Vancouver." In spite of the large corporations controlling most of the media, some stories are just too juicy to keep quiet. This one had all the ingredients—theft, forgery, murder, and the involvement of some of Vancouver's foremost families and art patrons.

Some enterprising reporter had tied Boyle's and Abramowitz's murders together. I watched Sheila Robertson with her lawyer making a statement about how she was an innocent victim of art fraud. Marian Clark's lawyer gave a "no comment" to a report that she had purchased stolen masterpieces for her personal collection. Five employees of the Vancouver Art Gallery were under arrest, as was a member of the Chamber's security force, and an employee of Feitler's Gallery, where I had delivered the recovered art to Chung. I was impressed both with the reporter who put it all together and with Inspector Fenton.

"Wil," I shouted. "Come see. Major art scandal in Vancouver. We're all over the news."

He came out of the bedroom dripping water and toweling his head.

"What are you yelling about? What about Vancouver?"

I pointed at the screen.

"Holy crap." He stood there, staring with his mouth open and making a puddle on the floor.

"I told you there was a leak," I said. "That day we got boxed by the trucks, and the day Reagan escaped. Two different leaks."

Just then, a picture of a woman came on the screen, and the announcer said, "Police are looking for this woman, believed to be the kingpin of the operation." It was Kieran Murphy.

I erupted in laughter. "Kingpin? Kieran? What idiots. Not a word anywhere about Reagan."

"I need to call Vancouver," Wil said and trotted into the bedroom. I followed and watched him grab his phone.

"What time is it there?" he asked.

"Like one or two o'clock in the freaking morning. No one is going to be awake. Here, give me that thing." I snatched the phone out of his hands. "Geez, you really need to get better equipment. I guarantee the people in your financial audit unit have better phones."

He glared at me, but I ignored it.

"Come with me," I said, and led him into the other bedroom where I had all my equipment set up. Taking a patch cord, I plugged it from a little gray box hooked to my network into his phone. "I assume you plan to call your people at the Chamber, and maybe Inspector Fenton?"

Wil nodded.

"Just plug this in before you call. This little box will encrypt your conversation so that no one can listen in. You know, like the media. The people that are broadcasting your quiet little investigation to the world."

"Okay. Thanks."

"You're welcome. Go dry off. Do you want some microwave quiche?"

⊕⊕⊕

Wil did talk to the local Chamber guys. In Ireland, the Chamber had taken over all major police functions. The Garda, the Irish national police, had been so corrupt that the Chamber abolished them along with the rest of the government in 2087.

A couple of hours later, one of Wil's Chamber contacts called him back.

"Murphy left the estate in Celbridge. She took a car and is driving toward Dublin," Wil said after he hung up.

"Is she alone?"

"Yeah. Our spotter said she put two suitcases and a backpack in the car, then left alone."

"She's running," I said. "Is Reagan at the estate?"

"We haven't seen him leave," Wil said. "Our information is that he's a night owl. Sleeps until almost noon."

"So, he may not know she's gone. Obviously, she doesn't feel as though he'll protect her," I said. We were walking along the south bank of the River Liffey. Stopping and looking north, I could see the steeple of Christchurch Cathedral jutting out of the water, and the ghosts of thousand-year-old buildings beneath the surface. So much of the history of the city had drowned. But not the airport, though it was much closer to being beachfront property than when it was built.

"You might stop her from getting on a plane," I said. "And if she drives past the airport, then she might go to her parents, who live about halfway between here and Belfast. And if she doesn't go to her parents' house, then she might be heading to the airport in Belfast."

"It might be more than a concern that Reagan

wouldn't protect her," Wil said as we turned up the hill into downtown and headed for Chamber headquarters. "She would probably be the most important witness against him. Men like Reagan aren't fond of witnesses."

At Chamber headquarters, we found Miles Callaghan—the Deputy Director of Criminal Investigations that Wil had been working with.

"We definitely have a runner," Miles said when we entered his office. "She's made it off the island."

"I thought you were watching for her at the airport," I blurted out.

Miles gave me a disapproving frown. "We were. She took a ferry."

I let that sink in. The only ferries I had any experience with were the ones that traversed Lake Ontario and the one in Vancouver.

"Why didn't security stop her there?" Wil asked.

Miles shook his head. "In North America, do you have security checkpoints to cross the street? There isn't any security. You drive into the ferry port, get in queue for your destination, pay the fee, and drive on board. Your girl probably knew the schedules, because within fifteen minutes of arriving at the port, five ferries launched."

He had a large map of Ireland on one wall. I walked over to it.

"Can we set a watch on the destination port?" I asked.

"Which one?" Miles countered. "If she took the shortest route to England, then she's almost there by now."

"Well, what are the possible destinations?" Wil asked.

"Isle of Man, Holyhead in England, Pembroke in Wales, Roscoff or Cherbourg in France. At the Isle of Man, she could get off, or continue on to Glasgow, or go to Belfast. From Pembroke, she could take a ferry back to Cork, or another to Cherbourg. From Cherbourg, she could go to Bristol or back to Ireland, and from Roscoff, she could take a ferry to Spain."

"We've lost her," Wil said.

"Unless we get uncommonly lucky," Miles agreed. "We'll have people watch the ports, but all it would take is for her to leave the car, wear a wig, and walk off the ferry. We'd probably never see her again."

"Yeah, if she was just trying to dodge us and the media, she might not take extensive precautions," I said. "But if she's running from Reagan, she's probably terrified. She could walk off the ferry with a backpack and two suitcases. That probably wouldn't be that unusual."

Miles nodded. "You're right, Miss Nelson. Most people who ride the ferries aren't bringing a car."

"So," I said, "since we can't watch everywhere, Wil, you take Roscoff, and I'll take Cherbourg. We fly there and wait for the ferry. We're the only ones who know her on sight, so we might have a chance of spotting her, no matter how she's disguised."

He gave me one of those patient smiles of his. "And why are you guessing France?"

"Because Murphy speaks French. She spent a year in France between university and graduate study, and another year doing an internship before she landed the job in Vancouver. You speak French, and I kinda do."

"Your Quebecois is good enough to get around in France," Wil said. "People might laugh at your accent, but they'll understand you. Most people speak

English, and all the Chamber people do."

"Great." I turned to Miles. "When can you give us a ride to France?"

CHAPTER 22

Either of the ferry routes from Dublin to France would take Kieran about nineteen hours. It took two hours to prepare a jetcopter for our trip, and two hours later they dropped me off in Cherbourg at the Chamber offices. I waved to Wil as they lifted off to take him on to Roscoff.

Wil arranged for me to get a Chamber car. I took it into the city and down to the port, where I took advantage and parked in an official reserved Chamber parking space. Before the bombing of Paris and The Fall, Cherbourg had been kind of a backwater. The Cherbourg that I found was a bustling, modern city with a huge commercial harbor and shipbuilding industry. The old historic city was underwater, including the ancient fortress the French and the English had fought over for centuries.

Checking my chrono, I saw that I still had ten hours to wait. With all that time on my hands, I asked around and found a seafood restaurant that several of the locals recommended. It took me some time to find it, and when I stood in front of the place, I wondered if they were laughing at the idiot tourist.

Bracing myself, I opened the door and stepped down into a dimly lit bar filled with the most incredible aromas and laughing, happy people. None of them looked like tourists, and none of them looked to be in danger of imminent food poisoning. I found a table, input my order through the automenu, and settled in to wait.

Wil called about an hour later. He'd landed in Roscoff, and a Chamber man he knew there was taking him out to dinner.

I sat and drank strong French coffee until I

realized I didn't need any more caffeine. I paid my tab and walked outside to wander around for a couple of hours. A pastry shop lured me in, and I bought a couple of eclairs.

The ferry port had a waiting area filled with people waiting to board, as well as those waiting for friends or family to arrive. I stood out on a narrow balcony overlooking the docks and leaned against the railing as the ferry from Dublin glided in and tied up.

I knew the make, color, and number of the car Kieran had taken, but I had a feeling she planned to ditch the car. The ferry dropped its ramp, opened its doors, and cars started driving off. At the same time, passengers began disembarking from a gangway on the side of the ship. I hadn't anticipated having to watch two separate exits, and I felt my neck starting to ache from swinging my head back and forth.

Then I saw her, walking down the gangplank. She wasn't wearing a wig, but she had her hair stuffed under a white knit hat so large that it looked like a bubble sitting on top of her head. Walking amongst several men much larger than she was, she wore a small backpack and carried two suitcases. Their bodies partially hid her, but also showed her height. She might have been smarter disembarking with a group of women.

I raced down the stairs and reached the bottom at the same time she walked into the terminal. Seeing her closer, I knew it was Kieran. She passed through the terminal and approached the taxi area. Most taxis were completely automated, but she approached one with a driver. She had a short discussion with him, and he loaded her bags in his trunk. As soon as they got in the car, I snuck up behind and attached a tracker to the bumper.

Whirling away, I ran to my borrowed car. The tracking app connected to my GPS, and I pulled out into traffic, following Kieran's taxi.

They drove across the city to the train station. The taxi driver drove like a madman, and if not for the tracker, I probably would have lost them. It was unusual to pay the extra for a driver, and I wondered if Kieran paid him even more for speed.

I morphed into my Jasmine Keller persona, abandoned the car in a no-parking zone, and ran into the station. When I didn't immediately see her, I panicked. After a search from one end of the terminal to the other, I decided that I had lost her.

Just as I was pulling out my phone to call Wil, Kieran came out of one of the washrooms. She walked over to the ticket windows and stood in line to buy a ticket. With a sigh of relief, I got in line behind her.

She bought a ticket in a private compartment to Lyon. When she walked away, I shoved my card into the machine and bought the same type of ticket.

"Please," I asked the guy behind the counter, "is my compartment near that woman's?" I pointed to Kieran's back.

He gave me kind of a weird look, but checked the computer readout. "Right next to it. Why?"

I made an expression of distaste. "She snores. She was on the ferry from England with me."

He chuckled. "I can move you to another car, if you wish, but you'd have to share a compartment."

"No, that's fine. I'll get some earplugs."

With a smile, he handed my ticket back and pointed behind me. "You really can't hear one compartment from another," he said, "but the shop over there sells all kinds of travel accessories, including earplugs."

I thanked him and called Wil. "She's here in Cherbourg, but she won't be here long. She plans to take a train to Lyon."

"Damn! Any way you can capture her first?"

"I don't think so. There are a ton of people. I mean, I might be able to get close enough to stick a gun in her ribs and steer her out of here, but what do I do if she says no? I'm not going to shoot her."

He was quiet for a bit while I tried to keep Kieran in sight. I really needed to get to that shop. I hadn't planned on a long trip, and other than having a toothbrush and toothpaste, I was woefully unprepared for an overnight.

"I can meet you in Lyon, or maybe someplace in between," Wil said.

"That works. Look, I've got an hour to get ready for a long train ride. I'll call you, okay?"

Luckily, Kieran went into the shop. While I was buying a package of underwear and other things, she bought two newspapers, a book, and a bag of chocolates. I added some chocolates and a newspaper to my purchases, too.

As I followed Kieran to our train, I reflected on how some words from the past seemed to hang on. Books and newspapers hadn't been printed on paper since long before I was born. To buy a newspaper, I laid my phone on a glass plate, then browsed on a screen for the media I wanted to buy. When I paid, a file was transferred to my device.

The compartment was similar to the ones I used in North America, and several steps above anything I had used on my previous trips to Europe. It even had a small sink and a toilet. Kieran obviously knew continental Europe better than I did. She had lived there for two or three years, and she had grown up in Ireland, so she probably had opportunities to travel around. I had spent two summers there when I was at university, and been to France, Germany, and Poland for jobs.

Although I saw Kieran get on the train and struggle getting her luggage into her compartment, I didn't trust her to stay there. As soon as I entered my compartment, I blurred my image, stepped back into the corridor, and plastered myself against the wall. I stayed there until the train lurched out of the station and began to pick up speed.

I attached a bug to Kieran's door and then went into my compartment. Sitting down on the bunk, I called Wil.

"Where are you?" he asked when he answered.

"On the train, heading to Lyon."

"Okay. I can get there before you do."

"Wil, we don't know if she plans to go all the way to Lyon. The train makes several stops."

He was quiet for what seemed a long time. "Wait," he suddenly said. "I know where she's going. She's going to Geneva."

It had been more than twenty-four hours since I got up and went running with Wil, so I was a little slow. Geneva? The word finally filtered through to a part of my mind not caught up in the moment. Switzerland, which still had a democratic government. Neutral, independent. Not run by the corporations. No Chamber of Commerce. Switzerland, where the government still regulated the corporations. Where any charges against her would have to be proven before we could take her into custody.

"Oh, hell," I said. "I'm so damned dense sometimes. Of course. Wil, I'm going to get some sleep. I'll call you when I wake up."

"Sweet dreams, Libby. I'll see you in Lyon."

I ate an éclair, brushed my teeth, and collapsed onto the bed.

⊕⊕⊕

The view out the window was dark when I awoke, though I could see occasional lights in the distance. I checked the time, then my GPS. We were approaching the city of Macon. The train would have a brief stopover, then the last leg to Lyon. I figured about an hour and a half.

Checking the route from Lyon to Geneva, I discovered that there wasn't a direct train from Lyon to Geneva. The train would go back to Macon, then change trains to Geneva.

Wil sounded groggy when he answered his phone.

"Where are you?" I asked.

"Lyon. I was just catching a couple of hours of sleep."

"Wil, she's not going to Lyon at all. She's planning to get off at Macon, and take a train from there to Geneva."

"Just a second." Silence, and then, "Crap. I should have checked the schedules."

"Me too. How long until you can get to Macon?"

"About an hour, maybe an hour and a half."

"We'll be gone. Go to Geneva."

I brushed my hair, ate my other éclair, and got ready to disembark. The next train to Geneva left in an hour, and I bought my ticket online. The bumping of luggage next door confirmed that my traveling companion was indeed getting off the train.

The train slowed and crept along through the outskirts as we reached the city and then into the station. I looked out the window and saw the city lights still in the distance.

At the sound of Kieran's door sliding open, I cracked my door and watched her pull her bags into the corridor. She turned her back on me and headed toward the door at the end of the car. Blurring my image, I followed her. A lot of people from our train got off.

Kieran briefly checked the notice board and took off toward the other side of the terminal. She clearly knew where she was going, walking quickly, but not appearing to be in a hurry. Since she didn't glance around or seem nervous, I assumed she didn't consider that someone was following her, let alone waiting for her.

Once again, she bought a newspaper. I hadn't even glanced at the one I had purchased, but to check on what she was reading, I bought one, too. While she sat on a bench and read hers, I stood in the shadows behind her and called Wil.

"Are you in Macon?" he asked.

"Yeah. The train leaves for Geneva in about forty-five minutes."

"I'm boarding a helicopter now," he said. "Any chance you can capture her before she crosses the border?"

The platform wasn't crowded, but there were a couple of dozen people near, and more coming.

"I'm not sure. Can you get some cops here to arrest her? I can impersonate a cop if you really want to get her."

I could tell he thought about it, but then he said, "No, don't do that. Just figure out a way to keep her off that train."

Pulling up the newspaper, I searched for the word 'art'. A dozen articles came up, three of which included Kieran's picture. For the most part, the articles focused on the culture of art collecting in Vancouver. One provided profiles of the Gallery's board of directors. I still couldn't find a single mention of Michael Reagan. I tried searching for his name and came up empty.

I tried to figure out what my options were. We had no idea of Kieran's plans once she reached Geneva. She probably had money stashed there, but she also might know someone in Switzerland who would help her.

I could take her if I ever got her away from crowds, but that would get trickier once we reached Switzerland. How would we get her back across the Swiss border? The Chamber had a guarded relationship with Swiss authorities, and the Swiss were notoriously picky about kidnapping people in their country. I couldn't imagine Wil taking any chance that would piss them off.

I waited fifteen minutes for Chamber security, feeling increasingly frustrated. On an impulse, I unblurred my form, walked over to Kieran, and sat down beside her. She gave me a quick glance, then did a double-take.

"Hi, Kieran."

"Libby. Uh, how unexpected."

"It is a long way from Vancouver. I tried calling, but you were very hard to catch." I nodded at the article she was reading on her phone. "You know, I warned you that you needed to get on the right side of that mess." I shrugged. "Of course, no one ever listens to me."

She stared at me, her eyes wide, and her mouth open as though she wanted to say something, but couldn't figure out what.

"I find it very interesting that Michael Reagan's name hasn't come up," I continued. "Don't you? I guess you don't have the money to pay people off the way he does."

I shifted my position to face her. "I never would have guessed that you're the brains behind the whole thing. I usually consider myself a good judge of character, but I just didn't think you were the kind of person who orders people killed in cold blood. Boyle, Abramowitz, Karen Schultz. How many more did you order O'Bannon to slaughter?"

"I-I didn't. That wasn't me. I didn't do that," she babbled.

I held up my hand and she stopped.

"Prove it," I said. She looked like I'd slapped her. "It's all your fault, Kieran." I motioned to her phone. "Stealing famous paintings. Defrauding rich people by selling them stolen paintings. And worst of all, forging famous paintings. You know that's the worst offense. Even the Swiss won't be able to protect you from that charge. You know what the forgeries do, don't you?"

She stared at me like a bird facing a snake.

"The forgeries disrupt the market," I said. "Collectors and insurance companies can deal with the thefts. But when no one can trust whether a painting is genuine, no one buys, and prices plummet. And someone who can copy a Rembrandt? A Monet? A Van Gogh? You'll never see the light of day again."

195

The train pulled into the station and stopped. Kieran looked in that direction.

"Look down," I said.

She turned back toward me and then looked down. The MiniStealth pistol I carried in my boot was in my right hand, its muzzle peeking out from under my left arm.

"If you take one step toward that train, I'll shoot you," I said.

Her eyes returned to my face, wider than before.

"What do you want me to do?" she asked in almost a whisper.

"Help me get Reagan and O'Bannon."

"If they don't kill me, what happens to me?"

"We tell the world that you were working undercover for the Chamber and NAI insurance. You walk away free under one condition."

"What?"

"If you ever even think of forging another painting, I'll hunt you down. You'll have to hold a paintbrush with your toes. Understand?"

She swallowed hard and nodded.

"Okay. We're going to sit here until someone comes to get us."

I pulled out my phone with my left hand. The muzzle of my pistol never wavered. "Wil? We didn't get on the train. Is someone coming to terminal three to collect us?"

"Us?" he asked.

"Kieran is going to cooperate. I offered her a deal."

"Oh, good God. I don't want to hear this, do I?"

"It's all good. Just hurry. This bench is uncomfortable."

⊕⊕⊕

CHAPTER 23

The train pulled out of the station. Kieran watched it go as though it contained all of her hopes and dreams. Two men wearing dark trousers and turtlenecks walked up to us. The older of the two flashed a Chamber ID. I could see at least three more security operatives hanging back.

"Kieran Murphy?"

She looked up at him. "Yes."

"I'm Investigator Durant. You're under arrest. Please come with us."

Kieran looked to me, and I nodded. We both stood. The younger man took her suitcases while Durant turned her around and slipped the backpack from her shoulders. Holding it, he turned to me.

"Elizabeth Nelson?"

"Yes."

"Director Wilberforce said that he will be here in about forty-five minutes. He'll meet us at the Chamber offices."

We all climbed into a car, Kieran and I taking seats in the back, and drove into the city. For some reason, the men in the front seat seemed to get more and more fidgety. When we reached our destination, the driver practically leaped out of the car, ripped open Kieran's door, and pulled her out of the car. Holding her tightly, he pushed her toward the building's door. Durant walked so close to me that he kept bumping into me.

The Chamber offices surprised me. I didn't expect such a large building in a small city.

"Pretty impressive headquarters," I said, staring

up at six stories of glass and steel.

"It is because of our proximity to the Swiss border," Durant said. He escorted us into the building and upstairs to a windowed room where they searched Kieran, rather too thoroughly, in my opinion. She didn't seem to mind, though. I couldn't hear them, but the expressions on their faces made it seem as though she was flirting with them.

"Is there a place anywhere close to get something to eat?" I asked.

"We have a cafeteria in the basement," Durant said. "There's a nice little bistro around the corner that is still open, and a pizza place across the street."

I didn't trust Kieran out of my sight. Durant gave me the number, and I ordered two pizzas. I noticed that both the younger investigator and Durant hung around the room where Kieran sat, watching her very closely and repeatedly going in to check on her.

The pizza was different than the pizza in North America, but it was good, and I was starving. When Wil walked in, there was only one slice left. He zeroed in on that slice and reached for it as he said, "Hi, Libby."

I slapped his hand. "That's my pizza." I picked it up and took a bite.

"Well, excuse me," he said, drawing back.

Pulling the second pizza from under my box, I handed it to him. He opened the box with a big smile.

"You do love me," he said, leaning over and kissing me on the cheek. He took a slice out of his box and bit off a third of it. I watched him wolf down half of the pizza before he stopped to breathe.

"I take it that you haven't been eating regularly," I said.

"Or sleeping. Where is she?"

I motioned toward the room where Kieran waited. Wil looked over, regarded her for a minute, then picked up another slice of pizza.

"Tell me about this deal you offered her," he said.

"I told her that if she helped us to take Reagan and O'Bannon and cleaned up all the forgeries, she could walk." I smiled. "I also told her that I would hunt her down if any more forgeries showed up."

Wil's expression didn't change as he listened, and when I finished speaking, he picked up another slice and took a bite. After the pizza was all gone, he said, "Complete cooperation, including testimony. She doesn't walk until it's all over."

I nodded. "But you'll exonerate her after that?"

"Yeah. We'll wipe her slate." He allowed himself a small smile. "The forgeries bother you more than the thefts, don't they?"

"Yes. I'm not sure why, but the fake paintings make me feel kind of sick to my stomach. I don't care who owns the originals, although I wish they were all where people could see them and enjoy their beauty. The fakes seem like a perversion somehow. They make me feel the same way as someone stealing food from children. It's just wrong." I shook my head. "That doesn't make any sense, does it?"

"Miss Nelson, you never cease to surprise me. How about we go see what Miss Murphy has to tell us?"

Kieran appeared appropriately nervous when we entered the room and sat down across the table from her. She fidgeted and wrung her hands. Exactly the same behavior as she'd shown when Inspector Fenton and I interviewed her in Vancouver.

Wil laid out the deal as he and I had discussed, then started asking her questions about the Gallery and Boyle, and the relationship between Boyle and Reagan. I found myself distracted by her expressions and body language. Just as in Vancouver, something about her felt off.

And something was causing me a weird kind of discomfort. It wasn't a sight, or a sound, or a scent, though when I glanced at Wil I saw his nostrils flaring. Then I noticed that his eyes were dilated, even though the light in the room was quite bright. My gaze fell to his lap, and I realized he was reacting to something very strongly. A flash of jealousy passed through my mind, which upset me even more.

I tried to isolate what was going on. The feeling I was experiencing was something I'd felt in the car with Kieran and Durant. It was similar to what I'd felt when Jon Cruikshank tried to scan me, but not exactly. Closer to what I had felt from a man named Gustav Alscher, a powerful projective empath who I once met in Chicago. He couldn't control me, but Wil was susceptible.

I leaned forward. "Kieran, stop it!"

She turned a beatific smile in my direction and batted her eyes. Wil gave me a rather glazed look.

I was tired and not in the mood for games. Grabbing her hair, I smashed her face into the table.

"I said, stop. Now."

The change in Wil's demeanor was immediate. He jumped up, upsetting his chair. I saw the glazed look fade from his eyes, to be replaced by a puzzled frown. The bulge in his trousers remained.

"Out," I said to him. When he simply stared at me, I pointed at the door. "Get out. Now." I stood, grabbed his shirt, and hauled him toward the door. "Get out," I repeated. "I'll explain later."

I closed the door behind him, then turned back to Kieran. She looked dazed. Her forehead was red, and blood poured from her nose. I stalked toward the table, and she shrunk down in her chair.

Leaning with both hands on the table, I said, "You keep playing games with me, and our deal is off. When I come back, you had better be prepared to explain what you just did. Understand me, Miss Mutant?"

When I joined Wil outside the room, I told him, "You need to assign only female guards for her. No interactions with men at all. If you want to interrogate her, you'll do it from outside the room."

"What's going on, Libby?"

"I'm not sure, but I have my suspicions." Pulling out my phone, I called Inspector Fenton.

"Hello?" Fenton said when he answered.

"Inspector, this is Elizabeth Nelson."

"Do you know what time it is?"

"Not really. I'm in France, and I'm not even sure what time it is here. I need to ask you about the informants you uncovered. The Chamber employee, the employee at Feitler's gallery, the one in your police force. Were any of them women?"

"No, all men."

"And who recruited them? Who was paying them?"

"No one paid them, as far as we can tell," Fenton said. "All three were involved with Kieran Murphy. She seems to have a talent for seducing men and getting them to do what she wants. So far, we have six men who have admitted to sexual relationships with her."

"Thank you, Inspector. Sorry to disturb you."

"Wait. Miss Nelson—" I hung up on him.

Wil stood watching me, rather impatiently.

"Set up the women guards for her and get a female doctor to see to her nose," I said. "Then let's go get a drink and we'll talk."

The bartender brought our drinks. I took a swallow of mine and leaned back in my seat, hoping my back and shoulders would relax.

"What's going on, Libby?" Wil asked.

"Nothing I can prove, but I'll bet my boobs that she's a mutant."

He didn't say anything for a couple of minutes, just stared off into space. "Okay. Go on."

"I spoke to Fenton. One of the reasons they think Kieran was at the heart of the art ring in Vancouver is that every time he turned around, he found her as the contact. She's the one who subverted all the informants. Fenton said she was screwing all of them—Boyle she told me about, Reagan I heard her with, one of your people, a guy at Feitler's Gallery, a cop—and Fenton said there were three more."

It was Wil's turn to take a large hit of his drink. "Very busy young lady. So, what does that have to do with her being a mutant?"

"There have always been reports of mutations that cause various hormonal imbalances," I said. "Some of those have to do with pheromones. Sexual attractants. Genetic femme fatales, you know? When I first talked with Kieran in Vancouver, she implied that Boyle was a mutant who used pheromones to seduce women. She tried to convince me that it wasn't her fault that she slept with him."

I chuckled. "She was simply laughing at me by telling me about her own abilities. I also strongly suspect that she's a projective empath, like Alscher, though not as strong."

"So, maybe Fenton was right, and she is the kingpin."

"That's stretching things. Reagan is twice her age, he's been a criminal his whole life, and he's richer than God. She may have used him, but she just took advantage of the situation."

Wil nodded. "Yeah. That makes more sense."

"Do you think we can find a room and get some sleep?" I asked. "We can deal with Kieran tomorrow."

"That, Miss Nelson, is the best idea I've heard in days."

Investigator Myra Madani was tall for a woman, though still shorter than me. She was about forty-five years old, with dark hair and eyes, and built like a truck. Durant introduced her to Wil and me, and said she was an empath. He called her 'a human lie detector.'

She and I met with Kieran the next morning. Kieran looked like crap, with a large bruise on her forehead, both eyes blackened, and her nose swollen and packed with gauze.

"Let's start with your mutation," I said. "Tell us about it."

Her eyes darted back and forth between Myra and me. We stared back at her without expression and waited.

Finally, Kieran said, "I don't entirely understand it. I've never told anyone about it, and no one has ever examined me. I just know that if I want to, I can have sex with any man I want, and they will do whatever I want them to."

"Any man? Any time?" I said.

"Yes. Young, old, rich, poor. It doesn't matter. I could walk out of here and screw Monsieur Durant in the middle of the lobby, and he wouldn't hesitate. Consequences be damned."

"And that's how you controlled Langston Boyle? How you got him to steal for you?"

"Huh? Oh, no. Langston was doing that long before I showed up. Michael just used me to communicate with him. You do know that Michael knew Langston before Vancouver. Michael paid for Langston's PhD."

I glanced at Myra, who nodded and said, "She believes what she is telling us."

"And how did you meet Michael Reagan?"

Kieran sighed. "I met Michael when I was an undergraduate. My parents didn't have any money, so I worked as an escort to pay for university. He became my sugar daddy, and paid for my graduate degree."

"When did you learn about your talents?" I asked out of curiosity.

"At puberty. Around fourteen. I couldn't control it at first, and it scared the hell out of me."

"When did you start painting for Reagan?"

"The copies? When he set me up in a condo with my own studio in Dublin. I think my style attracted him. He's obsessed with the impressionists." She shrugged one shoulder. "He used me, and I used him."

"Why did you go to Vancouver? Was it because Reagan was living there?"

"Only partly. Michael introduced me to Langston

in France. Michael already had the house on Vancouver Island, and he said he could help Langston get ahead at the museum. Langston wasn't averse to dealing in the shadows. His tastes far exceeded his salary. Michael introduced him to Marian Clark, and Langston hired me. The money we were making was incredible, and Michael was building an amazing collection for free."

"Was Langston sleeping with Marian?"

"Of course. Langston slept with everyone in a skirt. He slept with every woman on the Gallery's board of directors." Her lips quirked into a kind of a smile. "You didn't believe me about Langston and pheromones, did you?"

I shook my head.

"I wasn't lying about that," Kieran said. "I think he and I had the same mutation. Or at least something similar. We drove each other crazy. We had to avoid each other as much as we could. Barbara Willis caught us in his office, and I was afraid she would kill me. She was particularly susceptible to him." She stopped and seemed to study me. "And you weren't susceptible at all. Or were you lying?"

"Nope, not lying. He was a handsome man, but not my cup of tea."

Over the next four hours, Kieran outlined the entire conspiracy and all its players. I let myself fantasize a little. If we could corroborate some of what she told us, we could send half of Vancouver high society to the African salt mines. Of course, that would never happen, but we could use what she told us to coerce the rich into coughing up their stolen treasures.

Kieran verified that O'Bannon killed David Abramowitz and his granddaughter, giving us the day and time. Abramowitz had asked a few too many questions, and Kieran's boyfriend at Feitler's Gallery told her about the inquiries. She in turn told Reagan, who dispatched O'Bannon to find out why Abramowitz was curious. That led to the attempt on Danielle Kincaid.

"What about me?" I asked. "I'm sure Reagan wasn't happy about an insurance investigator showing up."

Kieran shook her head. "No, he wasn't. But Boyle had a partner we didn't know about, and O'Bannon got shot when he killed Boyle. He was in bad shape. Almost died, which I doubt anyone but Michael would have mourned."

For the first time, I learned that I had shattered O'Bannon's left shoulder, and put a bullet into his left lung. That corroborated what the innkeeper had told me. The fact that he still managed to reach his car and drive to a place Reagan's men could pick him up said a hell of a lot about how tough he was. Then he survived me shooting him again. I wondered if I should buy some silver bullets.

As it turned out, the combination of the news about the Vancouver Art Gallery and the news that O'Bannon was alive and traveling to Reagan's Castletown House was what spurred Kieran to run.

"With the scandal breaking, and the Chamber looking for me," Kieran said, "I became a liability. I didn't have to worry about Michael or any of his men killing me, but O'Bannon is immune. When I heard that he was coming to Celbridge, I assumed Michael called him to take care of me."

"Immune to your charms? Your pheromones?" I asked.

"Yes. O'Bannon is strange. He's some kind of

mutant, and I never got a rise out of him. He goes for either a certain type of woman, or pre-pubescent boys." An expression of disgust crossed her face and she shuddered. "I don't know what happens to his lovers, but Michael said something once. He said that Gavin isn't ever in a hurry. I don't know what all that applies to, and I sure as hell didn't ask. I just know that his women are there for a while, then they disappear, and no one ever sees them again."

"O'Bannon and Reagan have worked together a long time?"

"They've known each other a long time. Someone told me that they were kids together, but Michael is twenty years older than Gavin."

When we finished, I said, "You'll be coming back to Ireland with us." Kieran nodded. "Wil said that you'll be kept until we manage to bring Reagan and O'Bannon down."

"Good luck keeping Gavin in a cage," Kieran said. "You need to stake him in the heart and cut off his head."

I didn't say anything, but that made more sense than anything else she'd told us.

CHAPTER 24

The Chamber jet dropped out of the clouds over the Irish Sea, and we could see the coast of Ireland ahead of us. The battering the plane had taken while descending through the clouds intensified, and I silently cursed Wil for talking me into flying.

I had to admit that the private airplane was comfortable. Sitting in overstuffed chairs situated around coffee tables with a side table next to each chair was a lot better than being crammed into a tiny seat with no legroom and fighting for elbow space with the person next to you.

And it was fast. We covered the distance from Eastern France to Dublin in a fraction of the time trains and ferries would have taken. But trading speed for the prospect of an imminent death wasn't looking like a good bargain. The winds bounced the plane around like a madman's idea for a carnival ride.

"Are you okay?" Wil asked. He should have suspected I wasn't—by the white-knuckles of my left hand holding the armrest, or by the fact I was crushing his hand with my right.

"You'll pay for this," I said between clenched teeth.

"We'll be down in a few minutes," he said.

"That's what I'm afraid of. They say most passengers survive until the plane hits the ground."

A glance out the window showed a fishing trawler below fighting its way toward the shore through whitecaps taller than the ship. We had hit the storm just after passing over one of humanity's greatest monuments to stupidity. Much of Paris was still intact outside of the areas where the bombs had exploded.

The jihadis had set off a dozen incredibly dirty bombs, and the radiation levels were so high that scientists declared a fifty-mile exclusion zone around the city. The *Mona Lisa* still sat in the Louvre, but it was suicide to visit the museum.

The storm itself was the remnant of a hurricane that had ravished the east coast of North America. It hit the west coast of Ireland with one hundred twenty-five miles per hour winds and buckets of rain, but the pilot assured us that the flooding in Dublin didn't extend to the airport.

I think the Irish pilot's definition of flooding was different from mine. The plane splashed down and sent a huge wave of water flying up past the windows as we taxied into the hangar.

"Home sweet home," I said to Kieran as the plane came to a stop.

She gave me a sour look and said, "There are reasons why so many Irish people move abroad."

"You don't get that many hurricanes in Ireland," Wil said. His voice sounded a bit funny due to the filter plugs he wore in his nose to fend off Kieran's pheromones. She hadn't tried anything since I broke her nose, but we didn't trust her.

"So, are you putting me up in The Dublin?" she asked. The Dublin was a five-star luxury hotel.

Wil chuckled. "Even better. You'll have a suite on the fifteenth floor of Chamber headquarters. It has a lovely view of the bay."

We walked through a tunnel from the hangar into the airport terminal, then took a Chamber car to the headquarters building. The driver detoured around flooded streets several times. When we arrived, he stopped in front of the building.

"Have to let you off here," he said. "The parking garage under the building is sealed off to keep it from flooding."

It was only a short dash up thirty steps to the entrance door, but we were soaked by the time we got inside. A squad of female guards whisked Kieran away to her new digs, while Wil and I stood in the foyer and dripped.

"So, where are we going?" I asked. "All my clothes are at the townhouse, but I have no idea whether we can get there, or if it's dry."

He winked at me. "We are going to the hotel across the street. It's not The Dublin, but it is very nice, with a great restaurant and room service."

There was a tunnel, so I didn't have to get wet again. And he didn't lie about the quality of the food, which was delivered about the time I finished soaking in a nice, hot bath.

⊕⊕⊕

The following morning, while I waited for Wil to shower, I checked the news. To my surprise, the Vancouver art scandal was still on the front page, but for an unexpected reason. As soon as I heard the shower turn off, I called out to Wil.

He came into the main room of our suite, and I pointed to the screen. The day after Kieran ran, Michael Reagan had marched into Chamber headquarters in Dublin and filed charges against her for theft.

A quick search found the vid of the interview he had given the media shortly afterward. I about choked on the interviewer's introduction.

A blonde bimbo with a microphone said, "Michael Reagan, world famous art collector and

211

philanthropist, has revealed an event almost as shocking as the revelations out of Canada last week. A conspiracy at the world-famous Vancouver Art Gallery may have an Irish connection. Kieran Murphy, who is being sought for masterminding the thefts in Vancouver, once worked here in Dublin, according to Mr. Reagan."

The camera switched to Reagan. "I recently hired Miss Murphy to catalog my collection," he said. "Of course, I was as shocked as everyone else when the charges against her in Canada came to light. I checked and discovered several paintings, very valuable paintings I might add, are missing, as is Miss Murphy. I will be contacting the authorities in Canada as well. She spent considerable time at my Vancouver Island house, where she was supposed to catalog the portion of my collection that I keep there."

Wil shook his head. "There's no honor among thieves, is there?"

"Hey! Watch your tongue, mister. Just because those people are a bunch of lowlifes, it doesn't mean we all are."

He looked startled for a moment, then laughed. "I'm so sorry. Please forgive me. I promise never again to disparage the honor and customs of the illustrious Thieves Guild."

"Well, I wouldn't go that far. But you need to watch your stereotyping," I grumbled.

He kissed me on the top of the head and began to get dressed. "What do you want to do about breakfast?" he asked.

"Room service." I gestured to the window and the rain blowing sideways outside. "I'm waiting on some clothes to be delivered, but who knows when they'll get here with all of this going on."

"Who's bringing you clothes?"

"The store. I ordered them online. I can't go around dressed in a cat suit all the time. Some of your burglary boys might wonder."

"Can't you just, you know..." He wiggled his fingers.

I morphed into the image of Danielle Kincaid wearing a designer dress with pearls.

"Yes, I can do this, but I'd still be wearing a cat suit that needs washing and yesterday's undies. I'd rather be comfortable."

My clothes were delivered along with breakfast. We ate, then took the tunnel back to Chamber headquarters. I waited outside while Wil had a long meeting with his Irish counterpart. While the Chamber of Commerce was a world-wide organization, each main jurisdiction acted independently in local matters. Since charges had now been made against Kieran both in North America and in Ireland, Wil was afraid things might get tricky.

He came out of the meeting and smiled at me. "Not a problem," he said. "Let's go talk with Kieran."

Kieran's flat was much nicer than our hotel room. Obviously, it was kept for visiting Chamber executives who didn't want to lower themselves to staying in a five-star hotel. Wil handed her a list.

She glanced at it, then up at Wil. "What's this?"

"The list of paintings Michael Reagan said you stole from him."

She looked back at the list. "That sorry bastard." She closed her eyes, and for the first time I saw what I thought was genuine emotion on her face.

"Director Wilberforce," she said, "this is a list he made up to pull an insurance scam. Michael told me

213

that at one time or another, all of these had been owned by the various owners of Castletown House. They were either stolen before The Fall, were damaged or destroyed in some way, or they were quietly sold by previous owners to pay their bills. He had me sign authentication documents so he could insure them, then he planned to stage a burglary."

I looked over her shoulder and saw there were seven paintings on the list. None of them were world famous, though most were by recognizable artists. Reagan was smart, and he hadn't tried to do too much, but the scheme would probably pay him millions.

"And has he insured them?" Wil asked.

"Oh, hell yes. That was before I moved to Vancouver. Michael is a planner. It doesn't bother him to wait years for a payoff. He told the insurance company that the paintings were found in the attic."

"So, the paintings don't exist?"

"No, not a single one of them. At least not to my knowledge."

"But it does a hell of a good job of discrediting her," I said.

Wil nodded. "It certainly complicates things."

I sat down. "Kieran, are there any stolen or forged paintings at Castletown?"

"Unless he's moved them, there were when I left. At least a dozen that are on the Art Loss Database. Van Gogh's *A Wheatfield with Cypresses*—both the original and the forgery were there."

"If he did move them, where would he move them to?"

She thought for a while. "I guess it depends on what he's trying to do. I have a flat here in Dublin that he owns. If he wanted to implicate me, he could move them there." She got up, walked across the room, and poured herself a cup of coffee. Turning back to us, she said, "There's the house here in Dublin, and he has a house north of Galway. Not too many people know about it."

"What about O'Bannon's house near Cork?" I asked.

"I didn't know Gavin had a place near Cork."

"Okay," I said. "Now, you got out of the compound without any problem. What kind of security measures are in place?"

"The guards all know me, and they know the car I took. I just wave, and they open the gate for me." Further questioning about the estate's security revealed only that Kieran hadn't paid any attention at all to the systems or guards.

We left her rooms, so we could discuss what to do next.

"We can check all those other locations fairly easily," I said.

Wil shook his head. "Just because we have been out of town doesn't mean his estate wasn't covered. There hasn't been a truck large enough to carry a bunch of paintings leave his place since she did."

"So, they're still there."

"If she's telling the truth."

"We're back to sneaking me in there so I can verify there's a reason to go after him."

Wil didn't look happy, but he slowly nodded. "That might be our only option."

The Irish Museum of Modern Art was originally built as an English royal hospital in western part of the old city of Dublin. It was an impressive building, with an inner courtyard and surrounded by beautiful gardens. The Irish government had renovated it as a museum in the late twentieth century. As luck would have it, it was built on a hilltop, and after the oceans rose, it survived as an island.

The museum had a large fundraiser scheduled the following week. Wil set up an appointment with Madison McCrory, the director. Our goal was to talk her into inviting Reagan to give him an award for his generous support through the years. Chung promised a donation to fund the award.

"Flirt with her," I told him as I sent him out the door. I had checked, and the director was late forties, divorced, and good looking.

"Libby, I can't do that. I have to maintain my professionalism."

"Bullshit. Flirt with her. Don't ask her out or do anything you'll regret, but there's nothing wrong with being friendly."

He came back three hours later, smiling from ear to ear. "We're on," he said, holding up his thumb.

We knew when Reagan would be out of the house, and for about how long. With three to five hours, I could search the place completely. The problem remained as to how I would get in.

"Set me up with a car exactly like his," I told Wil, "and I'll go in as his chauffeur."

He shook his head. "Too risky."

"No, as soon as I park the car, I blend into the background. No one will see me."

Stubborn damned man. He called in some Irish

operatives to brainstorm.

"Have you ever done any skydiving?" one guy asked me.

"You mean jumping out of a perfectly good airplane hoping a piece of silk handkerchief will save my ass?"

Several of the people in the room chuckled, and the guy who made the suggestion said, "I'll take that as a no."

A woman asked, "Are you afraid of heights?"

Wil chuckled. "No, she isn't."

The woman got excited. "We could drop her on the roof with a glider."

"I could just bounce over the fence with a jet pack," I countered. "Look, I don't need any video science fiction stuff. When they open the gates for Reagan, a good distraction will do. I just slip in before they close the gates."

"Someone will see you and blow the whole operation."

They argued for a couple of hours. Eventually, I leaned back in my chair, crossed my arms over my chest, and gave Wil a look he should have been familiar with. He was. He thanked everyone and ushered them out of the room.

When he turned to me, I said, "Occam's razor. Create a distraction, and I'll use the front gate. Another distraction when he comes home. It's a no brainer."

"What kind of distraction?"

"I don't know. Something mundane that doesn't make them suspicious. Set off some firecrackers in the woods. Hire some local kids to do it. You can't tell me that Reagan doesn't have problems with the local kids pulling pranks. That fancy house almost demands it."

CHAPTER 25

The assassination attempt on Kieran Murphy shook the Irish Chamber's security division to its core. We had to piece together what happened after the fact, since everyone involved died.

As I kept telling Wil, no policing agency was totally clean. A man with Michael Reagan's wealth could always find someone to bribe, and there was a leak. In spite of classifying Kieran's presence at Chamber headquarters as 'need to know', too many people knew. The people who cooked her food and did her laundry might not have known her name, but they knew someone was sequestered away on the fifteenth floor. And people will gossip because other people will listen. I think it's baked into our genes. Without curiosity, we'd probably still be sleeping in caves and eating raw grubs.

Two men, dressed in security guard uniforms, made their way to the fifteenth floor. They could have taken either the elevator or the stairs, since they had legitimate key cards. Once there, they shot the guard stationed outside Kieran's door.

They next placed plastic explosive on the door and blew the lock. Then they tossed two fragmentation grenades through the open door. After the explosions, they entered the room and shot the two guards and the maid inside. That was probably unnecessary, but I guess the assassins wanted to make sure they didn't leave any witnesses.

At that point, they realized they had a problem. Faulty intelligence. Kieran wasn't there. She was down at the gym on the fourth floor with her other two guards.

Since they had been rather noisy, alarms sounded

throughout the building, and I guess they panicked.

After the hurricane passed, the weather settled down, and the floodwaters receded. Wil and I had gone back to staying at my townhouse. We were walking down the street toward the Chamber building after a late breakfast when we heard the alarms go off.

I hesitated, but Wil started to run toward the building. Grabbing his arm, I dragged him to a stop after a few feet and stepped in front of him.

"What is the matter with you?" I shouted with my face less than a foot from his. "You don't know what that's about. Use your bloody head." In some remote cranny of my mind I noted how different he and I were. My first reaction to an alarm was to get as far away as possible.

He craned his neck to look past me, and while he was distracted, I took the opportunity to pull him across the street.

"We can see better from here," I said. "Just hang on for a minute and let's see what's going on. If it's a fire or a bomb scare, you're not going to help anything by running in there."

People poured out of the building, primarily office workers and others wearing civilian clothes. No security personnel. That worried me. It meant something was going on inside.

Then two men in security uniforms emerged and struggled through the crowd of people. They gave the impression of being in a hurry, but they didn't seem to be chasing anyone.

"Wil." I grabbed his arm and pointed with my other hand. "Those two."

I took off running, and felt him beside me. The men broke free of the milling crowd just as I reached the one of them in the lead. I stuck out my leg and tripped him. He went down, and his buddy stumbled over him and sprawled onto the street, too.

One of them tangled my legs, and I went down hard, landing on my shoulder and biting my tongue. I saw stars as white pain lanced through me. I swallowed air, gritting my teeth and tasting blood, until the moment passed. Raising my head, I saw the man I had tripped roll over and point at me. I found myself staring at the business end of a pistol.

"Hey, man, I'm sorry. Okay? I'm just kind of clumsy," I said, scooting away from him on my butt.

He didn't shoot me. Instead, he took a look at his friend and started to scramble to his feet. My right arm was all pins and needles, so I drew a knife with my left hand. Even though I was at an awkward angle, I threw the knife, and it buried itself in the back of his thigh. He cried out and went down again.

The other man leaped to his feet. He raised his pistol toward me as I fought to get mine out of my bag. A shot rang out, and he jerked backward, his gun flying out of his hand, and fell to the street.

The man I had knifed raised his pistol toward Wil. I managed to free my pistol and shot the guy. I wanted to capture at least one of them, but as he slumped to the ground, I knew that plan had failed.

Wil and I both looked around, standing back-to-back. No one else appeared threatening, and at first, I didn't see any other security uniforms. A couple of minutes later, a phalanx of armed and uniformed personnel rushed from the building. Their behavior was completely different from the men who had just died. The security men fanned out, looking about and bracing for trouble.

Wil held his identification card above his head in

one hand, his pistol raised in the other, the muzzle pointed up. I raised my hands the same way. The last thing I wanted to do was get shot by my own side.

Several members of the security force approached us, took our guns, then checked our IDs. A couple checked on the two men we had shot. In both cases, I saw the guards shake their heads.

"Did you throw that knife left handed?" Wil asked as he helped me to my feet.

"Lucky throw. I was aiming for his back. I'm surprised I even hit him, let alone with the point."

After a thorough search of the building and vetting of everyone outside and inside, no other intruders were found.

"You've got a leak," I said when Wil and I were alone with the Irish security director and three of his top staff. "Reagan has someone inside who's paid to feed him information."

No one argued with me. They just looked unhappy.

In the discussion that followed, someone said, "It's too damned bad that O'Bannon escaped."

I let that one go, but when Wil and I were alone again, I told him, "O'Bannon didn't have anything to do with this. He has a reputation as the consummate professional, and this was the amateur hour from the word go."

"Maybe he still isn't completely recovered from his wound," Wil said.

"May be, but whoever planned this was an idiot. This operation was all brawn and no brains. Explosives, collateral casualties, no escape plan, and acting on faulty intelligence instead of scoping things out to make sure the situation was right. If O'Bannon wanted Kieran dead, she'd be dead."

Kieran wasn't happy, either. "You said you would protect me! Some protection. It's sheer luck that I'm still alive."

I agreed with her, but didn't say so.

She railed and ranted, throwing a tantrum worthy of a three-year-old or a diva. Having had no practice with the former, but a lot of practice with the latter, I walked out and let someone else deal with her. That someone else was the head of the women's jail. When I saw Kieran the next day, she was much calmer. I figured the new black eye probably had something to do with her change in attitude.

The surveillance team assigned to Reagan went on high alert. Wil said he half-expected the man to bolt. I wasn't that worried about it. In two more days, he had the chance to stand up in front of the cream of Irish society and accept an honor. The corporate aristocracy might normally look down on him, but in his mind, I was sure he felt the award elevated him to their level. He wouldn't miss the chance.

It did worry me that we didn't have a single reported sighting of Gavin O'Bannon. That evening, Wil had a conference call with his subordinates in North America, so I took a stroll.

O'Bannon's townhouse appeared as deserted as the first time I'd seen it. Bypassing the alarm, I entered and browsed through the place. Still no food in the refrigerator or any dirty laundry. But when I checked the gun safe, two of the pistols and the sniper rifle were gone. The missing rifle told me that he had plans. The chances of me using the Suri persona for anything plummeted past zero.

The investigation inside the Chamber ramped up to full-blown witch-hunt status. Everyone who might have spoken to anyone who knew about Kieran was interrogated in the presence of someone who was described to me as an empath-telepath.

I stayed as far away from the woman as I possibly could.

It turned out that one of the maids was sweet on a handsome young security guard and told him about the beautiful redhead hidden away on the fifteenth floor. He, in turn, told his buddy over a drink at the pub.

When Chamber security searched for the buddy, they didn't find him either at his home or work addresses. The guard was arrested for the security breach. The maid was sacked from her job, which was a type of prison sentence in itself. The chances she would ever find another corporate job with healthcare and other benefits were very slim. I knew she would probably lose her place to live, and the only jobs open to her would be those offered by independent businesses, paid hourly, with no benefits or protections at all.

Such personnel actions were always very public. The corporations, and especially the Chamber of Commerce, wanted employees to understand what complete loyalty meant.

"What's going to happen to him?" I asked Wil concerning the security guard.

His expression said that he wished I hadn't asked. "It depends. If they decide he was just young and stupid, he'll probably get a year in prison. If they decide he expected to profit from betraying us, then three to five years in a labor camp. If they charge him with conspiracy to commit murder, he'll get a needle."

Chamber headquarters had a few holding cells in the basement, but the main gaol, as the Irish called their prisons, was on the southern outskirts of the city. I wasn't there when the loose-mouthed guard was transported to the gaol, but later I learned that when he got out of the van at the gaol, he had his head blown off by a high-powered rifle.

I had strong suspicions as to who pulled the trigger.

The following day, the body of his friend from the pub was found in a rubbish bin in an alley in one of the poorest parts of town.

Reagan obviously didn't like loose ends.

CHAPTER 26

Wil dropped me off at the edge of the residential neighborhood near Reagan's estate in a light drizzling rain. I moved into the woods, blurred my form, and made my way to the wall surrounding his house. Clinging close to the wall, I slid along until I could see the gate.

Dropping down, I hugged the angle where the wall met the ground and crawled within a few feet of the opening. And then I waited. I didn't know when Reagan would leave for Dublin, but I knew what time the reception started. That would be followed by a dinner, a couple of speeches, and then Reagan would receive his award. An orchestra would play afterward so people could dance and arrange assignations, then he would come home. I would have about five hours.

Half an hour after I moved into position, the gates opened. Reagan's limo drove through, and then the driver slammed on the brakes to keep from hitting the motorcycle that suddenly appeared on the road.

That was my cue, and I wormed my way forward until I reached the driveway. The limo driver and guards at the gate watched as five more motorcycles drove by. And while they watched the motorcycles, I crawled through the gate and back along the inside of the wall. When I got about ten feet past the gatehouse, I stopped.

Looking back over my shoulder, I saw the limo disappear beyond the gate, then the gate closed. The guards meandered back to the guardhouse and shut the door against the rain.

Since Reagan installed his own security system, no plans were on file. I didn't know if there were pressure plates buried under the lawn inside the wall, but there would have been if I had designed the security. I crawled back along the wall, past the guardhouse, and along the edge of the driveway.

It was a long crawl in the rain. Halfway there, the sun set, and dusk fell. I stood and trotted in a crouch until I reached the house. Working my way around to the right, I came to the door on the right side, the one we had watched Kieran use when she went horseback riding.

It wasn't locked.

The sound of a vehicle off to my right caused me to crouch down and wait. A large truck with a twelve or fifteen foot covered back drove down the drive without its headlights. The guards opened the gate, and it left the compound.

Sneaking into the house, I cautiously made my way from room to room. The place was huge, but I had studied the floor plan. Each room was large, but the total number of rooms was small. Three rooms in particular had been designed for displaying art: the Pink Drawing Room, the Green Drawing Room, and the Long Gallery upstairs.

I crept down a long, dimly lit hallway, sliding along the wall to keep my silhouette from showing. I slipped through the door at the end and glanced to my left at the grand entrance hall. My townhouse in Toronto would have easily fit in the space.

Turning right into the Green Room, I immediately recognized that something was wrong. Paintings hung on about half of the available wall space. I continued through to the Pink Room, which obviously also had been stripped of artwork. I didn't see any paintings that looked newer than the eighteenth century, but Reagan was known for collecting late-nineteenth and early-twentieth century works.

I moved through the study and up the stairs to the Long Gallery. The murals there were famous, but there was plenty of wall space to hang paintings. I found only three.

After skulking through the rest of the house, I had to conclude that Reagan had fooled us. I hadn't seen a single painting that I could identify as stolen or a forgery. I also hadn't seen any people.

The bottom two floors seemed to be a nineteenth-century showplace. Like a museum. I knew the building to the west—connected by a portico—contained the kitchen and some servants' quarters. Like many Irish great houses, it didn't have a basement due to the high-water table. The third floor held bedrooms and bathrooms.

I had heard some noises from up there. That might be where O'Bannon was, but he wasn't an encounter I was ready for. I wanted a bazooka the next time I faced him.

I remembered Wil saying, "There hasn't been a truck large enough to carry a bunch of paintings leave Reagan's place." One had left that night, without lights, and I hadn't given it a second glance.

Making my way out of the house, I found a comfortable bench on the other side of the stables, under an eave out of the rain, and called Wil.

"Is everything okay?" he asked.

"Oh, yeah. Great. I haven't found any of the art I was looking for, but it's a very pretty house. Did you see a truck leave here?"

"No. Hang on a minute, let me check. Can you call me back in five?"

"Yeah, sure."

When I called him back, he said, "A truck drove

228

past and onto the highway about an hour ago. Why?"

"It came from the compound. It drove out with its lights off, and I just thought the driver was an idiot."

"Wait, it came from the house?"

"Yeah, and I'll bet it had all the art that isn't here. It looks as though the art on the walls came with the house when he bought it. If you raided this place right now, Reagan would sue your ass off."

Wil's cursing didn't hold a candle to my dad's, but he was a lot younger. I was still impressed. "So, what do we do now?" he asked after he wound down.

"I sit here and wait for them to open the gate again. I hope Reagan doesn't decide to spend the night in town."

Reagan must have had a good time, because he didn't leave the museum until midnight, and didn't get home until one o'clock in the morning. Wil called me when the limo pulled off the highway, and I slipped through the yard to the gate. When Reagan pulled into the compound, I crawled out.

After I trudged for half an hour through the woods, Wil picked me up and took my sorry butt home. My clothes were waterproof, but the temperature was in the sixties, and I was chilled to the bone. I lay in a hot bath and drank tea until I warmed up, then crawled into bed and let Wil warm me up some more. I couldn't remember spending a more miserable night.

⊕⊕⊕

"Wake up, Libby."

"Huh?"

"C'mon. Wake up. Kieran escaped."

"What? How?" I struggled to sit up and open my

229

eyes. Wil pressed a mug of coffee into my hands.

"I'm not sure. I just got the call. She's gone."

I took a sip of the coffee and tried to figure out what that meant for me. "Did she take her bags?" I asked.

"I don't know. Why?"

"Did anyone ever search her stuff?"

"I don't know. Didn't you?"

"No."

We got dressed and drove downtown. As soon as Wil parked the car, his phone rang. He listened, then turned to me. "Reagan just left Celbridge. According to the people monitoring the drone we have over there, O'Bannon and two of his chief enforcers were with him."

"You've got another leak. Either that, or she called him. But that doesn't make any sense."

Wil shook his head. "She couldn't get away from us the last time she ran. Maybe she thinks she can sweet talk him."

"He tried to kill her."

I sat around while Wil met with the Irish operatives engaged in the investigation. Wracking my brain, I couldn't figure out any kind of logic behind what was going on. Kieran's actions were so crazy that I couldn't even try to foresee what she would do next.

Wil found me while I was eating breakfast in the Chamber's cafeteria.

"It seems that no one ever searched Kieran's luggage," he said in greeting. "Everyone thought that someone else must have done it."

I rolled my eyes. "So, how did she escape?"

"She might have been kidnapped. Someone

gassed the gym with a non-lethal gas this morning. Kieran and the security guard regularly stationed there are gone."

"Male guard?"

With a disgusted expression, he said, "Yes."

"What took so long last night?" I asked. "I thought the festivities were supposed to be over around ten."

"They were."

"So, why did Reagan hang around until twelve? Did a lot of people stay after?"

He looked thoughtful. "I don't know. I didn't ask." Pulling out his phone, he called someone, and they spoke for about fifteen minutes.

"The only people still there were Reagan and the director, Madison McCrory. They left at the same time."

"Oh, crap. No wonder she was so accommodating. He's doing her."

Wil opened his mouth as though to protest my statement, but decided not to say anything.

Reagan went to his waterfront home in North Dublin. An hour later, his limo left, heading toward the airport. Half a dozen other cars also left, all going in different directions. The total number of cars overwhelmed the number of people and drones the Chamber had allocated to their surveillance.

As I watched the various screens in the surveillance center, and watched people scurrying around, talking to each other and to phones, I realized that we didn't know where Reagan was. The limo had pulled into a garage, and then back out again. No one saw Reagan get out of the car, or get back into it. The same applied to O'Bannon. It struck me that Reagan might know that Kieran was loose again, but he didn't know where.

If that was the case, we had dozens of Chamber assets plus dozens of syndicate assets running all over Dublin looking for one small woman who didn't want to be found. But Kieran really wasn't my problem, and neither was Reagan. I needed to find one painting and a sack full of jewelry.

I told Wil I was going shopping for a winter coat, which was a pretty flimsy excuse, and left. The bus took me to the Museum of Modern Art, where I paid my admission, and entered with the families, students, and tourists.

The building was enormous—a square surrounding a central park and a sculpture garden. It originally was built as a military hospital, and small rooms off the long corridors faced the interior courtyard. I estimated the chances of getting lost there at close to one hundred percent. A quick tour through the building to see all the stairways and doors closed to the public gave me a basic idea of the layout. The north wing of the building appeared to be a non-gallery space.

A painting in one of the rooms drew me to inspect it more closely. It wasn't one of Kieran's better efforts, but I assumed it was done much earlier than the paintings I'd seen in Vancouver. Sure enough, the plaque said it was donated by Michael Reagan.

When I walked past the gift shop, café, and bathrooms, I came to two glass doors that said, 'Administrative Offices.' On the other side of the doors, a receptionist and her desk provided a blockade against further progress.

Depending on how I wanted to approach Director McCrory, I could say I was a representative of NAI, or I could say I was Michael Reagan's wife, or I could sneak in. Option one, the legitimate way in, didn't fit my plan. I didn't want to give her any warning. And as much fun as the second option might have been, I chose option three.

Ducking into the ladies' room, I blurred my image and snuck back out into the corridor. I didn't know how often the door to the administrative wing opened, but I set myself up next to it and waited.

An hour later, a man walked out of the door, which swung outward, and I slipped through the opening. The receptionist barely noticed him leaving. I sidled along the wall around her desk. When I got behind her, I discovered she was chatting with someone via her computer. It must have been an interesting conversation, because her attention was riveted on her screen.

I wandered down the hall, checking the plates next to the doors. The center of that wing held a sumptuous ballroom and banquet room. I didn't find the director's office, so I climbed the stairs to the second floor. It kind of figured that she would have an office overlooking the fantastic gardens that spread out from the original main entrance.

I called Wil.

"Where are you?" he asked. "I've been trying to call you."

I figured that, but I had the phone turned off. "I'm at the museum. I'm going to mute your side, but leave the phone on. Just listen." I turned down the sound and put the phone in my pocket.

Morphing my clothing to a pink business suit, I unblurred and walked through McCrory's door. She looked up, and I saw an immediate flash of irritation on her face, quickly smoothed over.

"May I help you?" she asked.

"Yes. I'm wondering if you have any comment on the allegation that Michael Reagan was the center of the stolen art scandal at the Vancouver Art Gallery. Considering your personal intimate relationship with Mr. Reagan, and the fact that you honored him with an award the other evening, I'm sure questions about the collection here will soon be forthcoming. I thought you might want to get ahead of the issue."

"Who are you?"

"Dani Kildare, reporter for Irish News Tonight," I replied.

"Get out of here!"

"I don't think so." I sauntered across the office and sat down in a chair in front of her desk. "I assume you know what happened to Langston Boyle. Michael Reagan is rather ruthless in disposing of witnesses. And considering that he's been using the museum to launder forged paintings, I think you qualify as a witness."

She turned so pale I thought she might faint. "I don't know what you're talking about."

"Are you really that naïve? You have forgeries hanging in your galleries. What happened to the originals? I assume he split the profits with you."

I watched her hyperventilate, then suddenly she started scrabbling in her desk drawer. I leaped around the desk, expecting her to pull a gun, but when I grabbed her wrist, I saw she held a medicine bottle. Taking it from her, I shook one pill out and handed it to her. She stuck it under her tongue.

"I would imagine that prison or a work camp would be hard on someone with a heart condition," I said. She was sweating and pale, and her hands trembled. "It would probably be a good idea to cut a deal with the Chamber. At least, that's what I would do."

McCrory stared at me. The look of terror in her eyes told me that all intelligent thought had shut down. I'd seen the same look when I held a gun to someone's head. Time to back off. I walked around the desk and plopped back down in the chair.

We sat and stared at each other until her breathing slowed, and her face gained a bit of color.

The intercom on her desk buzzed. "Miss McCrory? Mister Reagan is here to see you."

CHAPTER 27

Pulling my pistol out of my bag, I pointed it at McCrory and motioned to the other doors in the room. "Which one is the loo, and which one is the closet?"

She blinked at me, then pointed to one of the doors. "That's the loo."

"If you tell him I was here, or give him any warning that anything is wrong, I'll kill both of you." I opened the closet and stepped inside.

While that was going on, the voice on the intercom said, "Miss McCrory? Mr. Reagan is waiting."

McCrory leaned forward, keyed the intercom, and said, "Send him in."

I blurred my form and stepped back out again as I closed the door. Standing very still with my back to the wall, I waited. Reagan came in and closed the door behind him.

"We have a problem," Reagan said. He stopped and scrutinized McCrory. "What's wrong?" Then he caught sight of the medicine bottle. "Are you all right?"

"Yes, I just had a moment," she said.

He walked around the desk, leaned down, and hugged her. "I'm sorry. I don't mean to stress you, but we have Kieran again."

McCrory's head jerked up. "Where is she? Does she..." She broke off her question as her eyes darted toward the closet. Reagan wasn't looking directly at her and didn't seem to notice.

"Did she have the jewels?" Reagan finished for her. "No, she stashed them somewhere."

236

"The Chamber—" McCrory started, but he cut her off.

"No, if they had them I'd know it. She stashed them before they picked her up. Don't worry, though. Gavin is on his way here. She'll tell him."

"Here?"

"Yes, she's downstairs, along with all my other secrets," Reagan said with a chuckle.

I hoped Wil was getting all of that.

"I need to make a shipment," Reagan said. "We're going to take your lorry to the airport."

"Are you sure this is a good time? You know, with the Chamber watching so closely?" McCrory asked.

"They don't suspect you," he said. "They didn't pay any attention to the truck the other night. Don't worry so much. I have everything under control. Now, are you feeling better?"

He helped her out of her chair and they walked to the door. She kept shooting glances back at the closet. I waited until they left the office and followed them.

McCrory was still shaky, and leaned against Reagan as they slowly walked toward the stairs.

"Michael," she said, "a woman came to see me. She knows, Michael. She said that we are running the same scheme here as you did in Vancouver. Selling originals and replacing them with forgeries."

He stopped. "What did she look like?"

"Very tall, blonde, probably late twenties."

"Elizabeth Nelson," he said. "Damn her! She was here?"

"This afternoon."

"I'll have Gavin deal with her," he said, and I felt a chill. "As soon as we get through with Kieran, I'll tell him. First we need to find that jewelry."

They took the stairs to the first floor, then through a door and down two more flights of stairs to a basement. The basement wasn't part of the original building. When the oceans started to rise, a philanthropist had teamed with the Irish government to build a seawall around the museum. They also dug out a basement under the structure, driving support pillars down to bedrock to prevent it from sinking.

The result was a large garage for parking cars and buses, as well as a temperature- and humidity-controlled vault for storage. Having never been there before, I discovered it was a maze. Numerous doors, seemingly randomly situated, indicated the presence of rooms.

Reagan and McCrory turned down a narrow hallway that turned at the end and led to one of those doorways. He punched a code into the keypad, and they entered the room. I rushed down the hall and caught the door before it closed. On the other side, Reagan pushed to close it. I stuck my foot in to hold it open and unblurred.

He pulled the door open again, an exasperated expression on his face. That expression turned to one of dismay as he saw me standing there with a gun pointed at him. He stumbled back a step, then backed away slowly. Beyond him, I saw Kieran, her hands cuffed together, hanging from a hook on the wall. Her feet didn't reach the floor.

Two men, both as tall as me and much bulkier, stood near her. A man in a Chamber uniform lay sprawled in a corner. From the looks of him, and the puddle of blood, I knew he wouldn't be getting up.

One of the thugs put his hand inside his jacket. I shot him and then shot the other man. Reagan took advantage of the distraction to rush to Kieran's side, draw a pistol, and point it at her head.

"Don't move, Nelson, or I'll kill her."

I met Kieran's eyes and raised my eyebrows. "After all those steamy nights together?" I asked. "You certainly aren't the kind of lover a girl dreams about."

It seemed as though I could feel the kind of buzzy feeling as I had when Kieran used her empathy, but maybe that was wishful thinking. I knew the men I shot seemed distracted, and their reactions were a bit slow. Reagan's eyes began to lose focus, so I kept talking.

"It's all over, Reagan. You've run out of options."

Kieran wriggled, spinning a bit, and he reached out to steady her. Reagan's gun wavered a bit, and I shot him in the forehead. He fell to my left, and the sound of his pistol exploded like a cannon in the small space. Kieran spun on her chain to my right.

I rushed to her, lifting her by the waist with one arm while I unhooked her shackles with my other hand. Laying her down on the floor, I inspected the wound on the side of her head and was relieved when I saw it was only a graze, maybe two inches long.

The sound of a woman running in heels drew my attention, and I saw McCrory's back as she disappeared through the door. I leaped up and chased after her. She reached the end of the hallway and burst out into the parking garage before I could catch her.

A couple of dozen people, some close to us and some at a distance, were looking our way. The sound of Reagan's gun had been quite loud, since it didn't have the built-in silencer mine did.

McCrory was already winding down, stumbling

and gasping for breath. And then beyond her, I saw O'Bannon walking toward us. He raised his hand, and I heard the soft spit of a silenced pistol. McCrory sprawled on the floor and lay still.

He turned his eyes upward to me, eyes that showed no emotion whatsoever. I blurred my form and dove forward as I fired. He dove to my left as he fired, hit the ground and rolled. Taking his cue, I rolled the same direction. When he stopped rolling, he fired three shots in the direction where he'd last seen me. I fired back, then rolled again, coming to a stop against a wall.

O'Bannon leaped to his feet and sprinted away. I fired at his back, but didn't see any indication that I hit him. He cut around one of the large pillars, and I caught a fleeting glance of him still running past it and then around the end of the wall I lay against.

I waited a moment. He had four options. If he snuck back and waited for me to move, he might see me. If I followed him, he might be waiting for me. He could continue to run, and either keep going or set up an ambush for me elsewhere.

Crawling my way along the wall, I passed the pillar and came to the corner where he had disappeared. In spite of being blurred and basically invisible, I inched forward, peeking around the corner and trying to expose as little of me as I could. He was heading for the stairs, but then he took a sharp turn toward the entrance ramp for cars.

I took off in that direction, too, hoping to gain ground on him and maybe cut him off.

He was almost to the opening when a Chamber car sped through, followed by several more cars. I had to dodge, diving to the side and rolling, as the lead car almost hit me. When I looked up, security forces spilled out of the cars. Some of the cars stopped outside, and more security personnel spread out. O'Bannon was nowhere to be seen.

Jumping to my feet, I raced for the entrance. Once I was outside, I saw O'Bannon running away to my left and immediately followed him. He was headed toward the gardens that spread out from the original front of the building. Four squares were filled with geometric patterns outlined by sidewalks, low and high hedges, and lines of trees planted close together. Beyond that was the old gatehouse.

Finding someone in the gardens wouldn't be easy. On the other hand, getting out of there wouldn't be easy for him, either. If not for a twenty-five-foot-high seawall, the entire garden would have been submerged.

I slowed to a trot and fished out my phone. "Wil, can you get a helicopter or a drone up over the gardens in front of the museum?" I waited, but Wil didn't reply. Frustrated, I looked at the phone and realized I'd turned the sound off. That was easy to fix. "Wil, can you hear me?"

"Hell, yes, I can hear you. I've been listening the whole time. Where are you?"

"Out front. Can you get a helicopter up? O'Bannon is going into the garden in the front of the building."

"Working on it."

I put the phone away and took off running again.

By the time I reached the beginning of the hedgerows, O'Bannon had dropped from sight. I realized that he could be within a stone's throw of me, but if he was lying behind one of the hedges, I wouldn't see him unless I circled around. The seawall showed the definite boundaries of the museum grounds, broken only by the road across the bridge that ended in the parking garage.

Slowing my pace, I cautiously moved along the south edge of the garden. The lawn was recently mowed, and the hedges were trimmed as square as boxes. I thanked all the gods I'd ever heard about that O'Bannon only had a pistol. With his marksmanship and a rifle, he could find a spot and hole up for days. The old gatehouse could provide such a spot. The only way to get him out of there would be with a missile.

My phone rang, and I dropped down behind a hedge before answering it.

"The copter's up," Wil said. "It should be here in a few minutes. What else can I do?"

"Surround the garden. If we can work our way from the outside in, he won't have any place to run. If he thinks he's cornered, he might give himself up. But if he thinks there's a chance to escape, God help anyone who gets in his way."

"Yeah. I know someone like that." His tone was dry and sardonic.

I sucked air. It hurt to hear him say that, but I knew he was right.

"Yeah, I don't give a damn about anyone but myself," I said.

"Libby, I didn't mean that the way it came out. I'm sorry."

"No. You're right. O'Bannon and I understand each other."

I thought I heard the sound of a helicopter in the distance. Chamber troops in SWAT gear ran crouched along the hedges to get into position. I unblurred my form. No sense in getting shot by friendly fire.

"Tell your men not to shoot any blondes," I said. "O'Bannon is bald as an egg."

"Where are you?"

"Right in front of the main entrance."

Someone shouted, and I stuck my head up. O'Bannon saw what we were doing. He leaped up from behind a hedge and sprinted down the sidewalk toward the old gatehouse. It was a long way to go, and I hoped the copter would get there in time to cut him off. I jumped up and followed him.

The copter swooped in, and a voice boomed out of a loudspeaker. "Stop! Drop your weapon and put your hands in the air." The copter's rear doors were open on both sides with mounted machine guns poking out.

O'Bannon stopped, turned, and looked up at the helicopter. He raised his hands in the air, but I noticed he didn't raise his left arm any higher than his shoulder. Then he brought his hands together, holding his pistol in a two-handed grip, and fired. The man behind the machine gun disappeared from sight.

As soon as O'Bannon fired, he wheeled and resumed running toward the gatehouse. I followed him.

The copter turned around, and the machine gun on the other side opened up. The hedges on both sides were only about four feet high, and O'Bannon threw himself off the path and over a hedge. Leaves from the hedge flew into the air as the bullets struck it, then the firing stopped. I assumed the gunner couldn't see his target anymore.

I didn't hear the shot, but I did hear the pop of the bullet passing by my head. Taking a page from O'Bannon's playbook, I vaulted over a hedge on the other side from where he had gone and hugged the ground, waiting for more bullets. None came, but I

243

wasn't sure if I was better off risking an inadvertent bullet while camouflaged, or a deliberate bullet by O'Bannon.

The machine gun hammered again, and I risked looking over the hedge to see where it was shooting. The copter was a lot closer to the gatehouse than it had been earlier.

Taking a chance, I blurred my form, jumped up, and raced in that direction. I didn't get back on the sidewalk, but ran on the grass, keeping close to the low hedge. I reached the end of the first large square and hurdled the hedge, but I didn't land clean. I stumbled and plowed face first into the hedge on the other side. Sharp pain erupted in my face and shoulder as the sharp ends of freshly trimmed branches jabbed me.

I drew back and saw a stick as big around as my pinkie dripping blood. A place just below my ear hurt like fire, and my hand came back with blood on it when I touched there. It was a wonder I hadn't put one or both of my eyes out.

Fighting my way to my feet, I tried to locate O'Bannon. The copter hovered in front of the gatehouse and sprayed fire at the entrance, then abruptly rose higher into the sky. O'Bannon had evidently found cover inside.

I unblurred my form and moved to my right toward the SWAT personnel converging from that direction. Behind them, I saw Wil moving toward me.

He trotted up and asked, "What happened to you? Are you all right? You're bleeding."

"I don't want to talk about it." Besides the sharp pain at my jaw, my whole face stung. He handed me a handkerchief, and I wiped my face, then pressed it to my jaw below my ear. When I held it up to look, it was half red.

"You look like you took a shotgun to the face," he said.

"Lovely. I take it that he went to ground?"

"Yeah, he went into the gatehouse."

"I suppose that firing a missile in there is out of the question."

He gave me a dry chuckle in response. "I don't think the locals would be very happy if we blew up a five-hundred-year-old landmark."

I studied the gatehouse, or what I could see of it from a hundred yards away. It had four round two-story stone towers with a brick house between them on the second level. It looked like the kind of place built to withstand a siege. "I guess I need to go in there and find him."

"Why you? We can gas him, or just starve him out."

"That's an idea."

Even as we spoke, a couple of men moved close to the house and fired gas canisters inside. They reloaded, and fired again and again, a total of ten rounds. The rest of the troops closed in and set up to wait. The gas filled the house and the towers. A standard filter mask, such as the ones we all wore, and that O'Bannon wore, would be overwhelmed by such an assault. Still, he didn't come out.

We waited for half an hour, after all the gas had dissipated.

"Got a gas mask?" I asked.

"You're going in there, aren't you? Do your invisibility thing?"

"O'Bannon doesn't know Reagan's dead."

Wil's brow scrunched up. He turned and looked back at the museum, then back to me. "What happened in there? We found a slaughterhouse."

"Reagan and his thugs are mine," I said. "Reagan shot Kieran, and O'Bannon shot McCrory, although I can't fathom why. She was a main part of their scheme." I shrugged. "Maybe Reagan thought she was a weak link."

"What about the Chamber man?" Wil asked.

"I don't know. He was dead when I got there. O'Bannon was late to the party. He shot McCrory, then he and I shot at each other, and we've been playing hide-and-seek ever since."

"So, explain to me again what you're planning to do?"

"Go in there as Reagan and talk O'Bannon into giving himself up."

He closed his eyes, and his lips moved, but I didn't hear anything. I couldn't decide if he was praying or counting to ten. Suddenly he reached out, pulled me to his chest, and hugged me so tight my ribs creaked.

"Be careful, Libby."

One of the Chamber men gave me a gas mask and a flak jacket. I circled around the gatehouse to come at it from the blind side. Carefully inching my way around one of the round towers, I fell to my knees and crawled through the gate. As soon as I was out of sight of those outside, I morphed into an illusion of Michael Reagan.

"Gavin!" I called. "Don't shoot. It's me."

I slowly walked through the door into one of the towers and began climbing the steps. "Gavin, can you hear me? Are you all right?"

When I reached the second level, I pushed the door into the main house and stepped through. "Gavin, it's me. Don't shoot." Someone coughed off to my left.

O'Bannon cautiously peeked out of the next room. He had found water someplace, soaked his jacket in it, and wrapped it around his head. Even so, his eyes were bloodshot, and he couldn't stop coughing.

"Gavin," I said, "give yourself up. They don't have any witnesses, and my lawyers will take care of things. We'll blame Kieran and Madison on the Nelson bitch."

O'Bannon stepped out into the open. "You're not Michael," he said, swinging his pistol toward me.

I fired three times as fast as my finger could pull the trigger, and all three shots hit him in the chest. Stepping closer but stopping just beyond arm's reach, I took careful aim and shot him in the head. Then I shot him again. Any surgeon who could scrape his brains up and put them back together would be a magician.

With a sigh of relief, I let the illusion go and took the stairs down to ground level.

"Hey, it's me, the blonde chick," I called. "Don't anyone shoot me, okay?"

"Stand down!" I heard Wil yell.

I peered around the corner, and didn't see anyone pointing an assault rifle my direction, so I stepped out into the open, both hands raised above my head and clearly visible.

"He's dead," I called. Several men immediately rushed past me and into the towers on both sides.

Wil walked over and looked me up and down. "No luck getting him to surrender?"

"Nope. He wasn't in a reasonable mood."

CHAPTER 28

"Did you find Kieran's bags?" I asked Wil as we walked back to the museum.

"Yeah, they were in that room where we found her. Someone searched them before we got there."

"And her backpack was there?"

"Backpack? No. Why?"

"Wil, when those guys blew up her room and killed her guards, did it look as though someone searched it?"

"Yes. The drawers were pulled out, closet ransacked, that sort of thing."

As soon as I could, I commandeered a ride back to Chamber headquarters. Kieran's old room was still shattered from explosions and murder. I spent about forty-five minutes going through it, looking for hiding places.

From there, I searched through her current room, which was across the hall. That took a lot longer, but again, I didn't come up with anything unusual. Her backpack was still missing.

Wil showed up about that time. "What are you looking for?"

"I'll let you know if I find it," I said.

He followed me down to the gym. Other than her room, that was about the only place she was allowed to go to. She was there during the first attempt on her life, and she was kidnapped from the gym that morning.

Faced with a main room five times the size of Kieran's suite—full of closets, equipment storage rooms, locker rooms, the pool, and the sauna—I took a deep breath. Two hours later, I had barely scratched the surface of possible hiding places when Wil came in and brought me a sandwich. His timing was great, as the grumbling in my stomach was starting to distract me.

After finishing my lunch, I passed through the locker room to the ladies' room. Just the site of all those lockers and linen closets was enough to think about a stiff drink. I could be searching the place for the next month.

Since I was there, I looked around the ladies' room. The only closet held toilet paper and cleaning supplies, but no backpack. I couldn't see any other hiding places. Then I opened the last stall, the only one with a real wall. A maintenance panel—a plate of metal—was screwed onto the wall with four screws. It had been painted over.

Closer inspection showed that the slots on the screws didn't have any paint. I dug out my Swiss army knife and removed the screws. The panel slid to the floor, revealing a hole with pipes and a cutoff valve for water to the room. And a small blue backpack. It felt rather heavy when I lifted it out.

Opening the pack up, I found the type of things a woman might put in a getaway bag. Tampons, brush, toothbrush and toothpaste, small makeup kit, extra undies, and a few other things. Nothing of great interest. But the bag seemed rather shallow. Emptying it out did almost nothing as far as reducing its weight. I found a zipper around the edge inside at the bottom, covered by a cloth flap.

In the bottom compartment, wrapped in foam and tape, the crown jewels of England and France lay hidden. Not all of them, of course, but enough to call it a king's ransom. The Princess of Wales Tiara, Queen

Elizabeth's ruby and diamond earrings, the Cullinan Yellow diamond set in a brooch, Queen Victoria's emerald necklace and earrings, Empress Marie-Louise's crown, and the Regent Diamond, plus half-a-dozen lesser rings, earrings, and loose stones.

I just sat for a few minutes, gazing in wonder at what I held in my hands. The Regent Diamond, pale blue and one hundred forty carats, had been insured for a hundred million credits. The French crown was literally priceless, but for insurance purposes it had been valued at a quarter of a billion credits.

Wil called my name and brought me back to reality. Carefully re-wrapping the jewelry, I put it back in the pack and took it with me.

"Is that the backpack you're so concerned about?" Wil asked.

"Yeah. About half a billion creds. Want to run away with me?"

He did a double-take. "How much?"

"Believe me, enough to buy you the best steak in Dublin, with two bottles of fancy wine, and have money left over."

⊕⊕⊕

I knew from experience that doctors had no appreciation for how long it took a girl to grow her hair out. I practically wanted to cry the following morning at the hospital when I saw Kieran with her head shaved. She was sitting up in bed, and to my surprise, she smiled at me.

"I was hoping you'd come," she said.

I stopped and took a step backward. "You aren't hiding anything sharp, are you?"

She laughed and held up her hands. "Nope. Not your fault I didn't duck quick enough." The smile faded. "I would have rather died than have O'Bannon torture me. But I knew you were going to kill Michael. I could see it in your eyes."

"Are you doing okay?" I asked. "I can't believe they shaved your head."

"The doctors only shaved part of it. I had a nurse finish the job this morning. No problem, it will grow back. Yeah, I'm okay. No one will tell me anything, though. What's going on? Am I going to a labor camp?"

She tried to smile as she said the last part, but her voice quivered and her eyes weren't smiling.

"Remember our deal in Macon?"

"Yeah."

"When you check out of the hospital, you're free to go anywhere you want. Just don't paint anything you're not supposed to."

Her eyes searched my face. "Seriously?"

"Yeah. It's over. O'Bannon's dead, and so is McCrory. I turned the jewelry over to the insurance company this morning. Fenton is dropping all charges against you in Vancouver."

I handed her my tablet and keyed the playback.

"The hero of this case is Kieran Murphy," Fenton's image on the screen said. "At great personal risk, she worked undercover to break one of the largest stolen art rings in the world. Our thanks go out to her."

The announcer went on to say how billions of credits of stolen art had been recovered. There was even a clip of Marian Clark talking about how she had been swindled by the thieves.

I thought Kieran's eyes might pop out of her head. "You're kidding." She keyed the playback again. When it finished, she handed the tablet back to me. "You found the jewelry?" I nodded. "You're the one who found it, right?" I nodded again. "I should have figured. You're some kind of magician."

She motioned toward the tablet. "Thanks. That's a hell of a lot more than I expected. More than I deserve."

"I keep my promises. You be sure and keep yours."

Kieran said, "I will."

As I turned to go, she said, "Libby, I don't completely understand. I'm a thief. Why are you so willing to let me slide?"

I winked at her. "Because I'm not a hypocrite." I handed her my business card. "If you're ever in Toronto, look me up."

"Libby? I'd love to paint you." I remembered her nudes in Vancouver.

"Without my clothes?"

"Both. With and without. You're so long. I'll bet you'd look smashing in an evening gown."

I chuckled. "Come visit and we'll talk about it. I do have someone I would love to get a portrait of."

"He is gorgeous." I knew she referred to Wil.

"Yeah, he is, but that's not who I mean. Ever heard of a singer named Nellie Barton?"

⊕⊕⊕

Wil waited for me outside Kieran's room.

"What's next on the agenda?" he asked. "Are we going back to Toronto?"

"In time. Don't you think we deserve a holiday? Maybe spend at least a couple of weeks here in Ireland playing tourist? I'm really not looking forward to getting on an airplane again."

252

"Sounds like a plan," he said. "I talked to Chung this morning. I guess you made out like a bandit on this job." He paused, blushed, then said, "So to speak."

"Oh, yeah. My treat. Between NAI, the other insurance companies, and a few trinkets I picked up along the way, I'm not hurting for creds."

As we walked out of the hospital, Wil said, "Funny thing. Inspector Fenton tells me that David Abramowitz had no heirs. But when they checked with his banks, they discovered that just before his death, he donated a hundred million credits to the Modigliani Foundation."

"Yeah. Isn't it amazing how many public-spirited people there are in the art world?"

He stopped. "You gave away a hundred million credits?"

"Sure. Easy come, easy go. What the hell else would I do with that much money? I can't figure out what all these billionaires are thinking. If I lived to be a hundred, I couldn't spend that much money."

We spent three days hiking in Killarney National Park, a couple of days on the Dingle Peninsula, seeing the sights and going deep-sea fishing one day, and a week in Galway. We took day trips to castles and abbeys and the Cliffs of Mohr, and spent the nights listening to music in the pubs, and making love. We traveled back to North America on a sub-orbital supersonic jet—my first experience on one of the frightfully expensive planes—but the lack of weather at super-high altitudes was worth it.

I arrived home to a stack of paperwork and a dozen security installation jobs. Some of the job requests were months old, but Dad had kept the clients on the hook, promising them the world if they didn't cancel. Some good press from the Vancouver fiasco that mentioned my name helped with that.

About six months after I got home, I received an email from Kieran.

I sent you a package.

The next day, the shipping company called. "Miss Nelson? We have a package for you, but there's no delivery address."

I told them to deliver it to my mom's hotel. I never gave out my home address. And then I promptly forgot about it because I had an appointment with a client that afternoon.

When I got out of the meeting with the client, I checked my phone and saw a message from my mom. I rode my bike over there and was greeted with a very large skinny shipping crate stamped 'Fragile'.

"I've already scanned it," Mom said. "No electronics, no explosives. Who do you know in Switzerland?"

I tore open the envelope attached. A single piece of paper said, *It's all your fault!*

That was ominous enough. Carefully peeling away the packaging, we discovered a four-foot by three-foot painting of Vancouver harbor from the viewpoint of the cliff edge at British Columbia University. It was absolutely stunning. I found another envelope inside the crate.

An advertisement for a show at an art gallery fell out. On the back of it, written by hand, was a note.

I have a one-woman show opening in Geneva in three months. You and your gorgeous man are invited. And bring that lady you want me to paint. - Kieran

254

If you enjoyed **Chameleon's Death Dance**, I hope you will take a few moments to leave a brief review on the site where you purchased your copy. It helps to share your experience with other readers. Potential readers depend on comments from people like you to help guide their purchasing decisions. Thank you for your time!

Get updates on new book releases, promotions, contests and giveaways! Sign up for my newsletter.

Other books by BR Kingsolver

The Chameleon Assassin Series
Chameleon Assassin
Chameleon Uncovered
Chameleon's Challenge
Chameleon's Death Dance

The Telepathic Clans Saga
The Succubus Gift
Succubus Unleashed
Broken Dolls
Succubus Rising
Succubus Ascendant

Other books
I'll Sing for my Dinner
Trust

Short Stories in Anthologies
Here, Kitty Kitty
Bellator

BRKingsolver.com
Facebook
Twitter